SEALING THE BARGAIN

Eleanor knew that her father had told Lord Randolph that he had to consummate his marriage to Eleanor to receive his reward. Thus it came as no surprise that the earl waited no longer than their wedding night to come to her room and begin to undo her nightgown.

"After all, my lady," he said, nudging the silk and lace so that it fell over her shoulders and down her arms, exposing her to the waist, "you are my wife."

But Eleanor then took the lord completely surprise by reaching up with both hands to undo his nightshirt and very deliberately draw it down over his shoulders.

"After all, my lord," she said, "you are my husband."

Eleanor was not a merchant's daughter for nothing. . . .

MARY BALOGH, who won the *Romantic Times* Award for Best New Regency Writer in 1985, has since become one of the genre's most popular and bestselling authors. She has since won four Waldenbook Awards and a B. Dalton Award for bestselling Regencies, and a *Romantic Times* Lifetime Achievement Award in 1989. She lives with her husband in Kipling, Saskatchewan, where she expresses her musical talents as a church organist and cantor.

A CHRISTMAS PROMISE

by

Mary Balogh

A SIGNET BOOK

SIGNET
Published by the Penguin Group
Penguin Books USA Inc., 375 Hudson Street,
New York, New York 10014, U.S.A.
Penguin Books Ltd, 27 Wrights Lane,
London W8 5TZ, England
Penguin Books Australia Ltd, Ringwood,
Victoria, Australia
Penguin Books Canada Ltd, 10 Alcorn Avenue,
Toronto, Ontario, Canada M4V 3B2
Penguin Books (N.Z.) Ltd, 182–190 Wairau Road,
Auckland 10, New Zealand

Penguin Books Ltd, Registered Offices:
Harmondsworth, Middlesex, England

First published by Signet, an imprint of New American Library,
a division of Penguin Books USA Inc.

First Printing, December, 1992
10 9 8 7 6 5 4 3 2 1

1

The Earl of Falloden glanced at the visiting card resting on the salver his butler held extended toward him. He frowned.

" 'Mr. Joseph Transome, coal merchant,' " he said. "Why the devil is a coal merchant calling upon me? Could you not have found out his business and sent him on his way, Starret?"

The butler exchanged a brief glance with the earl's valet. "He was most insistent, m'lord," he said. "He declared that he could divulge the purpose of his visit to no one but you. You wish me to say you are not at home, m'lord?"

"Yes," the earl said irritably, motioning his valet to hand him his neckcloth. He had just returned from a morning ride in the park that had done nothing to lift the gloom from his mind, that *could* do nothing to lift it. He was not in the mood for visitors.

The butler bowed stiffly from the waist and turned to leave his master's dressing room.

"Wait!" the earl said. He looked even more irritable as he tied his neckcloth in a hasty and simple knot despite the compressed lips of his disapproving valet. "The man is respectable, Starret? And he came to the front door?"

"He arrived in a carriage and four, m'lord," the man said.

The earl raised his eyebrows. "I had better see what the devil he wants," he said. "Show him into the salon, Starret."

"Yes, m'lord." The butler bowed again before withdrawing.

"A coal merchant," the earl said to his valet's reflected image. "What do you suppose he wants, eh, Crawley? To get me to change my supplier of coal for the winter? Who does supply it anyway? Well, I suppose I should go down and satisfy my curiosity. He came to the front door asking for me instead of to the back asking for Mrs. Lawford. Interesting, would you not say?"

But he did not wait for an answer. He strode from the room and descended the stairs to the hallway of his town house on Grosvenor Square. The gloom of an early November morning made it almost necessary to have lamps lit, he thought as he crossed the hall and waited for a footman to open the double doors into the salon. It was a day entirely in keeping with his general mood.

Mr. Joseph Transome, coal merchant, was a cit, he thought as the man turned from the window at the opening of the doors. He was as neatly and as expensively dressed as the earl himself, and altogether more fashionably. The earl had not been able to afford to keep up with the fashions for the past year, though most of that time he had been wearing mourning anyway. The only criticism he might make of the merchant's clothing was that it all looked as if it might be at least two sizes too large for the man. He was thin and angular, with a sharp, beaked face, from which eyes too dark and too large looked keenly at his host.

The earl nodded to him. "I am Falloden," he said. "What may I do for you?" He stiffened when the man did not immediately reply but looked him unhurriedly up and down and half smiled.

"You are a fine figure of a man, my lord, if you will forgive me for saying so," Mr. Transome said, rubbing his hands together. "Finer than I had been led to expect. That is good."

"I thank you," the earl said coldly. "Did you have any business you wished to discuss with me, sir?"

Mr. Transome laughed and continued to rub his hands together. "You would think it strange indeed if I had come for no other reason than to admire your appearance, my lord, now would you not?" he said. "But that is important to me too."

The earl pursed his lips, stood near the doors with his hands clasped at his back, and declined to offer his guest a seat.

"Perhaps I should come straight to the point, my lord," Mr. Transome said. "If the nobility is like the merchant classes, then time is money, as I always say. And time is not to be wasted on unnecessary chit-chat."

"My sentiments exactly," the earl said.

"It seems, my lord," the merchant said, continuing to rub his hands as if washing them and looking apologetically at the earl, "that you are indebted to me for a considerable sum."

"Indeed?" The earl raised his eyebrows and looked haughtily at his visitor. "A household bill not paid, sir? I shall have you conducted to my housekeeper without further delay."

"No, no." Mr. Transome raised a staying hand. "Trifling stuff that would be, my lord, beneath your notice and beneath mine. Nothing like that. Your principal seat, Grenfell Park in Hampshire, is heavily mortgaged, I do believe, my lord?"

The earl's eyes sharpened.

"And the house and estate are getting shabbier and more dilapidated by the year with the rent money not even sufficient to pay off the mortgage costs," Mr. Transome continued.

"I do not know where you get your information," the earl said, "but Grenfell Park is no concern of yours, sir. If you will excuse me, I have a busy morning planned."

"Doing what, my lord, if I might make so bold as to ask?" Mr. Transome said. "Visiting your tailor or your bootmaker? You rarely do either these days since your bills at their establishments are already so high that you have no chance of paying them. And you are, when all is said and done, an honorable man. Or so my sources say.''

''Mr. Transome.'' The earl's voice was icy. ''I must ask you to leave, sir.'' He turned toward the doors.

''And you never visit Tattersall's these days, my lord, or attend the races.'' The merchant ignored the opening doors. ''And you do not play deep at cards, already burdened as you are with gaming debts higher than you can hope to pay in your lifetime—though they are not your own, I might add in all fairness. And many of them debts owed to moneylenders my lord. It is not a good situation. I daresay you do not sleep peacefully at night.''

The earl closed the doors again and took a few steps across the room toward his visitor. ''Mr. Transome,'' he said, ''I take it there is some point to this impertinence. Would you kindly get to it before I throw you out of my house? And would you kindly inform me how I am in debt to you? Something my cousin's man of business knew nothing of?''

''Nothing like that, my lord,'' Mr. Transome said, his voice soothing. ''I daresay you know the full extent of your debts. And they are sufficient to weigh on your shoulders as heavily as that mountain did on that giant's shoulders. What's-his-name. I always liked that story.''

''Atlas,'' the earl said curtly. ''I wonder how heavily you will weigh on my shoulders, Mr. Transome, when I transport you to my door in a moment's time.''

The merchant chuckled. ''Not much, my lord,'' he said. ''Not much these days. You now owe me all those debts, my lord. I bought 'em all. Every last one of them.''

The earl froze. And strangely he did not doubt for a moment that the man spoke the truth. All those debts his cousin and predecessor had incurred in eight years as Earl of Falloden. Those debts he had refused to repudiate when he had inherited fourteen months before. And he had refused to sell Grenfell Park with its vast estates because it had been his childhood home.

Because it was in his blood, a part of him, his most treasured possession. A millstone about his neck.

"Why?" he asked, his eyes narrowing.

"Why did I buy 'em?" Mr. Transome asked. "To do you a favor, my lord. It is better, less confusing, I always think, to owe money all in one place than all over London and the southern counties. Would you not agree, my lord?"

"I find the thought enormously comforting," the earl said. "So you have come to put the squeeze on me, Transome? You are going to have to wait. I will pay off every penny of the debt eventually. But it will take time."

Mr. Transome laughed. "I have worked hard all my life, my lord," he said. "Through diligence and a little good luck too, I have amassed almost everything a man could want in this life. Only one thing I have very little of, and it is the very commodity you ask of me. Time. I have very little time."

"Then," the earl said, "I shall have to reconcile my mind to debtors' prison, I suppose. I am sorry, sir, but I cannot reach into a pocket and bring out the sum I owe you. I wish I could. Believe me."

"I do, my lord," the merchant said, resuming his old occupation of rubbing his hands together. "But your debts can be canceled in a moment, my lord."

The earl smiled arctically.

"You scratch my back and I'll scratch yours, so to speak," Mr. Transome said. "You do something for me, my lord, and I'll cancel your debt. Every last penny of it. And make sure that you have the wherewithal to make of Grenfell Park one of the showpieces of England and its farms the most prosperous. And to spend some time and money at your tailor's again."

The earl raised his eyebrows.

"You are waiting to hear what it is you must do for me," Mr. Transome said. "It is a small something, my lord, in exchange for what you will get in return. But it will mean a great deal to me."

The earl did not change his expression.

"I will cancel your debts and settle half of my fortune on you, my lord—and it is a considerable fortune," the man said, "if you will marry my daughter. And most of the remaining half of my fortune will be hers after my death and so in effect will be yours too."

The Earl of Falloden stared in disbelief at his visitor. "You want me to marry your daughter," he said faintly, wondering for a moment if he had walked into some strange dream. A cit's daughter. A coal merchant's daughter. A total stranger.

"She is nineteen years old and a beauty, even if I do say so myself," Mr. Transome said. "And if it is refinement you want, my lord, you cannot do better than my Ellie. I had her educated at Miss Tweedsmuir's academy. Two lords' daughters were there at the same time and a colonel's daughter too. She was particular friends with Lord Hutchins' girl."

"How do you know I am not married already?" the earl asked coldly. "No, disregard that question. I do not have a doubt that you know everything about my life, sir. Doubtless you know of my attachment, though not betrothal, to Miss Dorothea Lovestone. Doubtless you know of the mistress I have had in keeping for a year past."

"Miss Alice Freeman," Mr. Transome said. "And a beauty she is too, if you don't mind my saying so, my lord. She is a credit to your good taste. But then so will Ellie be. You will have her beauty and her refinement and education and half my fortune, my lord. And she will be your countess. She will bear you the heir to Grenfell Park and your earldom. It is all I ask, my lord." He chuckled. "To be grandfather to an earl."

"Mr. Transome," the earl said quietly, "get out of my house."

The merchant scratched his balding head. "I understand that you are a man of pride, my lord," he said. "What member of the peerage is not? And I know that it goes against the grain, so to speak, to consider marrying into the merchant classes. But sometimes necessity must swallow up pride. I really cannot see that you have any alternative to what I have suggested.''

''Debtors' prison,'' the earl said curtly. ''That is an alternative, sir.''

''You have not even seen my Ellie,'' Mr. Transome said. ''How can you be sure you would prefer prison, my lord? And I cannot believe you serious. It is bravado. But even without prison, what is there ahead of you in life? You have not been able to offer for Miss Lovestone, have you, my lord, even though you have the title to dangle in front of her papa's eyes? You are too proud to offer her marriage while you are debt-ridden. But if you will pardon me for saying so, you will be an old man or perhaps even a man in his grave before you are free to offer. It is doubtful that her papa would accept you anyway since he is not himself a wealthy man.''

''My relationship with Miss Lovestone is entirely my own concern,'' the earl said.

''Quite so,'' his visitor agreed. ''But you were the first to mention her name, my lord. Let me be brief, since I see that you are eager to bring this interview to an end. You must marry my daughter within the month, my lord, or I shall call in my debts within the same month. I would hate to do it, but business is business.''

The earl set his hand on the knob of a door. ''Allow me to show you out,'' he said.

''I shall call tomorrow, my lord,'' Mr. Transome said. ''I cannot wait any longer. I trust you will think carefully of your decision.''

''There is nothing to think of,'' the earl said, opening the doors and motioning his guest to precede him into the hallway. ''You will be wasting your time returning here, sir. I will bid you a good morning.''

''Until tomorrow, then, my lord,'' Mr. Transome said, taking his coat and hat from a footman. ''I believe that in the course of one whole day and one whole night you will see that in all wisdom you have only one possible course. And it will be a good one, I can promise you. I have chosen you with care, since I will be entrusting to you my dearest fortune of all.''

''Good day to you, sir,'' the earl said, and he nodded to the footman to open the door and turned away himself to climb the stairs.

He felt rather, he thought, as a condemned man must feel when climbing the steps to the scaffold.

Eleanor Transome was no longer reading the letter that lay open on her lap. She was seated sideways on the window seat in her bedchamber, her legs drawn up before her, staring out at the dreary November day. But she saw nothing.

That was that, then. Wilfred did not want her. He did not love her. Oh, he said in his letter that he both wanted and loved her. He said it more than once. He said that he would always love her and always want her. But he would not marry her.

His reason was a noble one. He would not take her from the life of luxury to which she was accustomed, he wrote, in order to make her the wife of a struggling shipping clerk who might never make his fortune. And he would not accept help from her father even if it were offered.

''A man has his pride, Ellie,'' he had written—she had read the letter enough times already to have it memorized. ''And in some ways pride is stronger than love, for I would be consumed with shame if I begged your father for you with a sizable dowry and owed everything to him instead of to my own efforts.''

Eleanor closed her eyes. Men and their pride! She had written to him, improper as it was for her to make the move, explaining the situation to him, begging him to believe that she loved him, that for her love was all, that fortune and position meant nothing. After all, he had already expressed his intention of marrying her at some time in the future.

''I must set you free,'' he had written. ''I would have worked and waited forever to deserve you, Ellie.

But everything is changed now. I am sorry about your father. I had not realized that things were quite so bad. But he has tried to make provision for you. You had better bow to his wishes. At least you will be set for life—as you have been accustomed to be and as you deserve to be. Forget me, Ellie. Pretend in your mind and in your heart that I never existed."

But he had concluded the letter with a passionate affirmation of his love for her and an assurance that she would be in his heart every moment for the rest of his life.

She knew it was hopeless. Dear proud, foolish Wilfred. She knew that she would never succeed in changing his mind. And so he was lost to her, because she was rich and he was poor. Although they were second cousins. Perhaps because they were second cousins. Papa disapproved of Wilfred and his father because they had not been as successful as he. And Papa had always opposed her growing attachment to Wilfred, fanned by frequent meetings at family gatherings, calling it puppy love, chucking her under the chin and assuring her that he had far more satisfactory plans for her than marriage to Wilfred.

There was an earl. Eleanor still had her eyes closed. She let her head drop sideways so that her temple rested against a cold pane of the window. She did not know his name or anything at all about him except that Papa had set about netting him for her and was confident of success. That meant that he would succeed. Papa always did when he set his mind to something.

Papa wanted her to marry an earl. A member of the peerage. A member of the *ton*. She shuddered and remembered all the humiliation of the summer two years before spent in the country with her school friend Pamela, Lord Hutchins' daughter. She had been seventeen, fresh from school, eager for life and for fun and for love, and quite unconcerned about the fact that she was different in one essential way from every other guest. She had never even heard the word "cit" before that summer. But she had come to know it well, and to know that it was her nickname among the guests and that it was a derogatory term. It meant that she was a member of a lower class, an upstart class, a vulgar class. She had seen nothing but disdain in the eyes of the other ladies and contempt in the eyes of the gentlemen—except that the gentlemen had also assumed that a cit would be freer with her favors than a lady. Eleanor shuddered again, in part at the way she had reacted to it all—fighting back with instinct more than reason.

Papa wanted her to marry an earl. And the trouble was that she would not have the heart to say no. Not now. If Wilfred had replied differently, perhaps she would have made a stand. Undoubtedly, she would have made a stand. But without Wilfred there seemed no point in anything. Certainly not in defiance. And how could she defy a dying father who had been everything to her through her life?

Eleanor bit her lip, but unbidden tears squeezed between her eyelids anyway. Papa wanted so badly to see her well settled before he died. It had always been the pinnacle of ambition for him, he had told her just a few weeks before—the conversation that had prompted her letter to Wilfred—to marry her into the nobility, into the landed classes. He would die a happy man, he had assured her, if he could see her become a lady, which was what he had trained her all her life to become.

Perhaps Papa did not realize, she thought, that only one thing could create a lady—birth. She might marry a dozen earls, but she would still be a cit. For all of the rest of her life she would be despised. She did not want to be despised. She wanted to be loved. It was all she had ever wanted. Just simply to be loved. Was it a great deal to ask?

Obviously it was. She spread her hand over the letter on her lap without looking down at it.

Wilfred!

But the sound she had been half listening for reached her at that moment and put an abrupt end to her painful thoughts and her self-pity. She jumped to her feet and raced from her room and down the stairs to find that the person who had entered the house was indeed her father. Looking stooped and gaunt and exhausted.

"Papa," she said, waving away the servant and setting her arms up about her father's neck to kiss him gently. She knew better than to hug him tightly and cause him pain. "You should not have gone out. Oh, you know you should not. You are so tired. Come into the parlor and I shall fetch you a stool for your feet and a blanket for your legs. And I shall have some tea brought up to be taken with your medicine."

While she spoke, she undid the buttons of his greatcoat and lifted the garment gently from his shoulders, careful not to bump against him. She smiled cheerfully at him.

"I'll be sitting down and lying down long enough, Ellie," he said. "And it is a good morning's work I have done. One more tomorrow and all will be settled."

"As if other people could not conduct your business for you," she scolded, linking her arm lightly through his and leading him into the warm parlor and to the large blanket-draped chair beside the fire. "Papa, you should rest more. And you are in pain. I can tell by the fixed smile on your face. It is well over an hour past the time for your medicine."

"Medicines dull the mind as well as the pain," he said, lowering himself carefully into the chair and setting his head back with closed eyes. "All will be settled by tomorrow, Ellie. And then I can die with an easy mind."

"Don't talk like that," she said, smoothing the thin hair back from his brow and kissing it before fetching the stool for his feet and lifting them carefully onto it. "All you need is rest, Papa."

"Ah, the time for make-believe is past, Ellie," he said, opening his eyes to smile wanly at her. "Ring for tea, then. That carriage ride seemed interminable.

Tomorrow the earl will agree to my terms and I shall see the two of you married before I die.''

She made no protests. She had made enough during the past month, ever since Papa's physicians had finally admitted to him, on his insistence, that the cancer he had was killing him and was not progressing slowly. The time for protests was over, especially now that she had heard from Wilfred.

''What are your terms?'' she asked quietly, ringing the bell for the tray to be brought in.

''All his debts paid and half my fortune,'' he said. ''He has a huge estate and one of the finest mansions and parks in England, Ellie. With my money he can restore it to magnificence. And you will be his countess. Tomorrow it will be all arranged and then I shall die a happy man.''

She said nothing but stood quietly before the fire, looking down at him. It was hard to believe that just a few months before he had been a vigorous, robust man, who had appeared to be the picture of health. Now all his flesh had fallen away. His cheeks were sunken and his eyes were hollow. His breath was coming in rasping gasps. She knew he was in great pain and silently willed the servants to come quickly with the medicine that would dull it for a few hours.

So she was to be married for her money. But of course there was no other reason why a peer of the realm would marry someone from her class. She had known that all along. But she was to be married to an impecunious man who had lived carelessly enough to incur great debts—she had no doubt that they must be great if he was being induced to marry the daughter of a cit, sight unseen. A man who would despise her as the unpleasant but necessary means by which he had extricated himself from trouble. And a man who would waste the fortune Papa had worked hard a lifetime to amass.

Sometimes, she thought, it felt as if she had been dealt a death sentence just as surely as Papa had.

2

"You are foxed, Randolph." Sir Albert Hagley stood over his friend, grinning. "Better let me get you home, old chap."

The Earl of Falloden swirled the dregs of brandy in his glass but did not down them. Yes, he was foxed—for the first time since he could not remember when. He could not afford to drink anything in great quantities these days, except perhaps water. But unfortunately he was not foxed enough. Only his bodily movements were impaired. He set the glass down carefully on the table in front of him and congratulated himself on accomplishing the task safely. His mind was as lucid as it had been when he had arrived at White's a number of hours before.

"Come on." Someone was hauling firmly at his elbow, and he obeyed the pressure and swayed to his feet.

"So what would you do, Bertie?" he asked an indeterminate number of minutes later. He could not quite remember how he had left the club and got himself into his friend's carriage. But there he was, and he was contemplating his boots resting on the seat opposite. It was unmannerly to put one's boots on the cushions of someone else's carriage. The earl hiccuped and crossed his feet at the ankles.

"Oh." Sir Albert blew out air from puffed cheeks. "What would I do? Marry the chit, I suppose. I don't see that you have much choice."

"That is what he said too." He must have spilled a drop of his drink, the earl thought. There was a dull spot on the high sheen of his left boot. Had he told Bertie the whole story? He must have, he supposed. Had he told anyone else? He hoped he had not been entertaining a whole roomful of White's members with the tale of his woes.

"I've never even set eyes on her," he said. "And I'm supposed to marry her within the month. Did I tell you he's a cit, Bertie? A coal merchant? Do you suppose I should just take a gun to my temple and end it all?"

"For the dozenth time, no," his friend said hastily. "I really think I had better stay with you tonight, Randolph. I've never seen you so far into your cups. There's no knowing what you will do. Why not just sell Grenfell Park? You would make something over and above the mortgage and be able to pay off that bastard's other debts, though I fail to see why you should. And then you would be as free as you were when you were plain Randolph Pierce. That's what you ought to do."

The earl stared at his boots for a long while. "It's been in the family for over two hundred years, though," he said. "It was once my grandfather's. I grew up there. I'm fond of the place."

"Well, then," Sir Albert said, "you will just have to marry the girl, cit or not. Though it's a damnable shame, I must admit. Are you going to have to be listening to a cockney accent at your breakfast table for the rest of your life, Randolph? But you won't have to live with her, will you? Your life can proceed more or less as usual except that you will have the blunt with which to live well. And you will still have Alice."

"And a damned cit for a father-in-law," the earl said, grimacing. "And a damned cit for a wife. Her father says she is a beauty."

"He would," Sir Albert said.

"She was at school with Hutchins' daughter," the earl said, frowning. "Which one would that be?"

"How old is the girl?" Sir Albert asked.

"Damned if I know." The earl frowned in thought.

"Not quite twenty. He said that, I am almost sure. At least she is not long in the tooth, Bertie."

"That will be Pamela, then," Sir Albert said. "The third daughter. Hutchins had his eye on me for her a couple of years ago, but she is too horsey for my tastes. Had me out to a damned dull party in the country for almost a whole month. Wait a minute." He looked sharply at the earl. "What is this chit's name?"

"Good Lord." The motion of the carriage was making the earl's stomach feel decidedly queasy. "Don't ask me. Something Transome. Aggy, Addy, Ellie, Emmy—something like that."

"Be damned if she isn't the cit that Pamela brought home from school with her just to defy her mother over something," Sir Albert said. "Lord, she was an embarrassment. As vulgar as they come. Cockney accent, loud laugh, the whole show. She was out for a noble husband even in those days. Unfortunately for her, there were no takers. I'm sure her name was something like that, though we always just called her the cit. Hutchins was like a damned thundercloud."

The Earl of Falloden frowned and yawned. "Grenfell could be all mine," he said. "I could have the house and the park restored and the cottages repaired and make some of those hundred and one improvements my steward is always talking about. If I put a bullet in my brain, I couldn't do any of it, could I, Bertie?"

"No," his friend said. "Don't nod off to sleep, Randolph, there's a good chap. There's nothing worse than having to carry a drunken dead weight from carriage to house."

The earl settled his chin more comfortably against his chest. "And as you said, Bertie, I wouldn't have to live with her, would I?" he said.

"No, Randolph, old chap, you wouldn't," Sir Albert said. *"Don't go to sleep.* There is not far to go."

"Except to get my heir on her at some time in the future," the earl said.

"Plenty of time for that," his friend said. "You aren't even thirty yet."

"I'll leave her here for Christmas," the earl said. "She will want to be near her father and friends anyway. I'll go out to Grenfell. Come with me, Bertie? We'll have a spot of shooting. I'll invite some other fellows too."

"You already did," Sir Albert said. "At least half a dozen of them."

"Did I?" the earl asked. "For Christmas? It is settled, then. Perhaps Dorothea will come too."

"It would not be appropriate, old chap," Sir Albert said. And then he peered more closely at his friend. But he did not need the evidence of his eyes. The sounds coming rhythmically from the earl's chest were unmistakably snores. Sir Albert swore.

Mr. Joseph Transome had been offered a seat, unlike the morning before. But the Earl of Falloden stood before the fire, his hands behind him, not even feeling the direct heat at his back. He had a headache, and his stomach was not feeling as settled as he would have liked it to feel. And yet he almost welcomed his physical discomfort. It kept his mind occupied.

Mr. Transome was rubbing his hands together. "I am delighted that you have made the sensible decision, my lord," he said. "I was quite sure that on reflection you would."

"I believe it would be best to have the wedding in the spring," the earl said stiffly. "I have already invited guests—all male—to Grenfell Park for Christmas."

"Begging your pardon, my lord," Mr. Transome said, "but the nuptials must be within the month. In fact, within the week. By special license. I have it all arranged."

The earl raised his eyebrows. "By special license, sir?" he said.

"I want to see my Ellie well settled," his guest

said. "That must be done soon, my lord. I do not have much time." He smiled.

The earl looked at him in incomprehension and saw again the too-loose clothes on the spare frame, the hollowed cheeks and over-large eyes, the pallor.

"It is doubtful that I will see Christmas," Mr. Transome said. "Very doubtful. The chances are that I will not even see December, my lord." He chuckled. "My physician declares that it is only through sheer stubbornness that I have seen November."

The earl said nothing. There was only discomfort to be felt in the face of imminent death.

"I had to settle my affairs," Mr. Transome said. "That is what has kept me going, my lord. We will have the marriage agreement signed this morning, if you please. My lawyer has all the necessary papers outside. I know you are a gentleman, my lord, and will keep to your side of the agreement once it is made. But still I have a hankering to see with my own eyes Ellie settled for life. I will know she is happy once I see her become the Countess of Falloden."

The earl's lips compressed.

"The financial settlement I outlined to you yesterday, my lord," Mr. Transome said. "My lawyer will discuss it in greater detail in a moment. But two points are not in the written agreement and are important to me. I will have your word on them as a gentleman."

"And the two points are?" The earl spoke quietly. The blood was beating through his temples rather as if someone had placed a clock there.

"The marriage must be consummated," Mr. Transome said, smiling apologetically. "On your wedding night, my lord. I want to die without the fear in my mind that perhaps at some future date there will be grounds for an annulment of your marriage."

"An agreement is an agreement," the earl said. "I would allow no such thing to happen, sir."

"Nevertheless." Mr. Transome continued to smile. "I will have your word, my lord."

"Your daughter will become my wife in every sense

of the word on our wedding night,'' the earl said curtly.
''And the other point?''

''You will live in the same house as my daughter for
at least the first year of your marriage,'' Mr. Transome
said. ''I will not be alive to hold you to your word on
that, my lord, but I know how much honor means to
a gentleman. I know you will keep your word once it
is given.''

There was a lengthy pause. ''You have my word,''
the earl said quietly at last. ''Are you all right, sir?''

''Just a spasm.'' Mr. Transome held up one staying
hand while the other was spread over his stomach. ''If
you would be so good as to have my lawyer brought
in now, my lord, he will go over the details with you
while I sit here. It should not take long.''

The earl reached out and pulled the bell rope.

''You have made me a happy man,'' Mr. Transome
said.

The earl said nothing but merely nodded to his butler when the door opened so that the man who had
waited in the hall might be admitted.

Half an hour later it was all done. The Earl of Falloden had affixed his signature to the marriage agreement after having paid very little attention to the
explanations made by the lawyer. If it was to be done,
it would be done, and to the devil with the details, he
thought. They were thoroughly distasteful to him. Only
one thing caught his notice. Mr. Transome's fortune,
of which he was to receive half on his marriage to
Miss Eleanor Transome, was many times larger than
he had dreamed. Even the half of it would make him
one of the wealthiest gentlemen in England.

Mr. Transome got slowly to his feet when it was all
over. There was a stoop to his body that had not been
there the day before or that morning when he had arrived. He extended a hand to the earl.

''You will not regret this day's dealings, my lord,''
he said. ''And you will come to realize that my daughter is a greater treasure than the other riches that will
become yours on your wedding day.''

After a brief hesitation, the Earl of Falloden placed his hand in the thin one stretched out to him.

"I will expect you to call this afternoon, then, to make your formal offer to my daughter?" Mr. Transome asked.

The earl bowed.

And that was that. Two minutes later he was alone in the salon, staring down at his copy of the agreement. Within a week he was to be married to a girl he had not yet seen. To a cit's daughter. To a loud and vulgar creature, if she did indeed turn out to be Bertie's cit. And for the basest of all reasons. He was marrying her for her money and she was marrying him for his title and his position in the *ton*. He smiled arctically. The girl would soon discover that it was not so easy to break into the ranks of his class. Though perhaps she would not notice. She probably did not have a sensitive bone in her body.

Within a week he was to bed the girl and to live with her for a full year thereafter. So much for his plans to leave her in town while he went into the country for Christmas with Bertie and whoever else he had invited when in his cups the night before. But even without the promise, by Christmas she would be entirely dependent upon him for protection. Her father would be dead.

The earl clamped his teeth together and turned sharply to the door until he realized that there was nowhere he could go to escape what he had just agreed to. Damnation, he thought. Oh, damnation! And he wished for one moment that his cousin, the former earl, were still alive so that he could have the pleasure of killing him.

He thought of Dorothea Lovestone—the delicate and delectable Dorothea—with whom he had been in love for almost a year. She would be at the Prewetts' that evening. And he would be there too—to inform her in the line of polite conversation that he was betrothed.

Betrothed! Good Lord, he thought, glancing at the clock on the mantel, twenty-six hours before he had never even heard of Mr. Joseph Transome and his precious Ellie. Yesterday he had been merely miserable over his hopeless financial situation. Yesterday he had not know what misery was.

Well, now he knew. And by God, Miss Eleanor Transome would know too before Christmas came and went. By God she would. And yet, he thought, his hands opening and closing into fists at his sides, it was against himself his anger should be directed. He felt disgust and shame at what he was doing. He was marrying for money.

She stood in front of the parlor window, her back to it. She felt cold, but she would not move closer to the fire. She wanted to be as far from the door as possible. She wanted to see him clearly when he came into the room. She did not want him upon her before she could even catch her breath.

He had arrived already, she knew. She had heard the bustle in the hallway more than five minutes before. He would be sent to the parlor soon. There could not be much for Papa to say to him. All the business had been conducted that morning. He would be sent—Papa would not bring him. He had almost collapsed when he arrived home and was sitting now in a large chair in his study, moved in there several weeks before so that he could carry on with business almost as usual. He should be upstairs in bed, but she knew he would not go there until this day's business was all over with.

She would not sit. She did not want to be caught at a disadvantage when he came into the room. She stood motionless before the window. And then there was a tap on the door and it opened.

He was a harsh and a proud man, she decided in an instant first impression. There was a set to his face and his jaw and a lift to his chin and a glint in his eye that all proclaimed he was less than pleased with the situation. He would have been far better pleased to take Papa's money without being saddled with her into the bargain, she thought. And her own chin rose an inch.

He was also a handsome man, his hair a dark brown and slightly over-long, his features regular, his eyes blue. He was not particularly tall, but he was muscular and slim all at the same time—and in all the right places. The sort of man who lived an idle life and spent that idleness in riding and boxing and otherwise exercising his body in useless ways. He was an earl, she reminded herself—one of the idle and haughty rich. Except that he was not rich. He was a spendthrift and probably a gamer. She held her shoulders back and looked him steadily in the eye.

He was more handsome than Wilfred.

"Miss Transome?" he said, and ice dripped from both words, or so she fancied.

Who else could she be? She said nothing and deliberately did not sink into the curtsy that she knew the occasion called for.

"Falloden, at your service, ma'am," he said, making her an elegant bow. "Randolph Pierce."

Pierce. She would be Eleanor Pierce, she thought, testing the name curiously in her mind. His name was Randolph. Papa had mentioned only his title. As if there were no person behind it. But then perhaps there was not.

She did not respond to his bow.

He came a few steps closer across the room and she could estimate that the top of her head would reach his mouth if he stood right against her. The thought turned her a little colder.

"I have your father's permission to call on you," he said. His face looked even harsher now that he was closer and the light from the window was shining full on it. And his eyes looked bluer.

Yes, of course. What foolish words. Why else would he be there? She knew that this moment must be as difficult for him as it was for her, but she would not make his task easier. Oh, she would not. He could never in a million years earn the fortune that Papa had

worked for all his life and that was to be given him
with only one encumbrance—her. Let him feel at least
a moment's discomfort.

"I have the honor of asking you to be my wife," he
said.

"Yes," she said at last. "Of course. And my answer
is yes. Of course." She was proud of the chill contempt in her voice. She would not add the words "my
lord." All the training of her school years and the
years before that at home with a governess prompted
her to do so and to drop into that curtsy she had neglected on his entrance. The occasion called for the
words. But she would not say them. He was not her
lord. Not yet, at least.

He looked at her with his harsh, set face as if he did
not quite know how to proceed. She felt a moment of
triumph and no sympathy for him at all. And no discomfort on her own account. She did not care if ten
minutes passed without another word being exchanged
between them.

"Then I am a fortunate man," he said, making her
another bow and reaching out his right hand.

It was a slim, long-fingered hand, well-manicured.
The hand of an aristocrat. She looked at it for several
moments before finally placing her own in it. But it
was a warm and surprisingly strong hand, she thought
as it closed about hers. And then he was lifting her
hand to his lips—warm lips—and her eyes traveled over
their hands and upward to his eyes. They were very
blue and very cold and held hers as steadily as hers
held his.

He hated her as she hated him, she thought. Good.
That was good. Let him suffer for Papa's money.

"I understand," he said, "that your father wishes
the nuptials to be celebrated next week. Will that suit
you, ma'am?"

"Of course," she said. As if it would make any
difference to anything if she said no. "If we wait any
longer, my father will be dead. Even as it is, he may
not live long enough."

The flicker in his eyes showed that he was somewhat taken aback by the frankness of her words. "I am sorry about your father's health," he said. "It must be distressing to you."

How could he know anything about her or what distressed her? He cared for nothing but getting his hands on Papa's fortune. Papa would not have been so rash with it or so hasty and unconsidered in his plans for her future if he were not dying. "We must all die sooner or later," she said.

"Yes." If it was possible for him to look colder, he looked it as he uttered the one word. "Next week it will be, then, ma'am. I have plans to spend Christmas in the country, but all will depend upon your father's health, of course."

"He will not last nearly so long," she said, and she held herself still and frozen, speaking as a matter of simple fact what the past months and weeks had shown her to be the harrowing truth. Papa was already living on borrowed time. Only his strong will would keep him alive until after the wedding. She was quite sure that he would live that long. But not many days longer.

"Well, then," he said, taking a step back and clasping his hands behind him. His eyes swept over her from head to foot. "Everything seems to have been settled satisfactorily. Shall we proceed to your father's study? He wishes to see us both after this interview is over."

He removed one arm from his back and was about to offer it to her, she knew. But she swept past him to the door, waiting for him to reach past her to open it only because it would have been too vulgar a breach of good manners to have opened it herself. She led the way across the hallway, nodding to a servant as she did so to open the door into her father's study.

"Well, children," her father said, opening his eyes. He was reclined back in his chair. "Together, are you? All is settled, then?"

"Miss Transome has consented to be my wife, sir," the earl's voice said stiffly from behind her.

Papa had had his medicine only an hour before. But he was still in pain, she could see. The knowledge chilled and frightened her. What would they do if the medicine became ineffective? He smiled and held out his arms to her.

"My darling girl," he said. "Come and be hugged."

But they were words from the old days. He had forgotten that she could no longer hug him or climb onto his lap as she had used to do all through her childhood at the end of a long day to tell him about her own day's activities. She could no longer touch him with more than the lightest of touches. She crossed the room and set her hand on one arm of the chair before leaning over and kissing him gently on the forehead. He dropped his arms.

"You should be in bed, Papa," she said, and her words sounded cold and abrupt, she thought. And she knew why. The Earl of Falloden was standing quietly a few feet away and she felt self-conscious.

Her father chuckled. "But this calls for a celebration," he said. "Ring the bell, Ellie, and we will have the tea tray and a decanter brought in. It is not every day that my only daughter becomes betrothed to a peer of the realm."

"Papa," she said, and she could still hear coldness in her voice, "you need rest."

"I must be taking my leave, if you will excuse me, sir," the Earl of Falloden said in a voice that quite matched her own—what a strange betrothal day! she thought—"I have a pressing appointment."

With his tailor, doubtless, she thought, or his jeweler. Or with his barber.

"Ah," her father said, holding out his hand to the earl. "We must let you go then, my lord. Must we not, Ellie?"

She watched him flinch in a manner perhaps observable only to her own eyes as the earl took his hand in a firm clasp. And she allowed relief to flood through her when her father instructed her to summon a servant to show their visitor out. She was not, then, to be given that task herself.

They were not to meet again, it seemed, until they came together at church the following week for their wedding. They were to be man and wife, she thought in some bewilderment as she watched him bow and take his leave. They were to live together in the intimacy of marriage for the rest of their lives—this stranger from a class she hated and she from a class he despised. She resolutely held her thoughts away from Wilfred.

"Ellie." Her father extended a hand to her, and she took it carefully in both her own and lifted it against her cheek. "Now I can die a happy man. Not quite yet, though. I'll live until your wedding day and perhaps a day or two longer. But you must not mourn for me very long. I have done all that I wanted in this life and more. And I will know that you have a life of security and respect and happiness ahead. I am well blessed."

"Papa," she said, turning her face so that she could kiss his hand and setting it down carefully in his lap again. And she blinked her eyes determinedly. There would be time enough to weep. But not now. "Let me help you to your room. You will be more comfortable when you are lying down."

"I think you are right," he said. "I'll go now, then. Is he handsome enough for you, eh, Ellie? They don't come much handsomer with a title and a large country estate to boot." He chuckled. "My Ellie a countess. And he is a young man—not even ten years older than you. Better than Lord Henley that I had my eye on for a while. He is almost my age. Are you happy, girl?"

"I will be happier when you are in bed," she said severely.

He chuckled.

3

She was a cold fish, the Earl of Falloden thought as he left Mr. Transome's house. And the same thought chilled him during the coming week, when he saw nothing of his prospective bride and father-in-law but carried on with his usual activities almost as if nothing extraordinary was happening to his life. It all seemed unreal until acquaintances began to comment on his betrothal and some even congratulated him and he discovered the announcement in the *Morning Post*.

He was about to be married to a cold fish. He shuddered at the memory of his interview with her. He had expected warmth, excitement, triumph, gratitude, chatter, vulgarity—something. He had expected something. Not the silence and the immobility and the thrust-out chin and the look of contempt in her eyes.

But why? She was getting what she wanted, was she not? She was getting her precious title and her *entrée* into society. Perhaps it was that she felt him enough her victim—and she was perfectly correct in that—that she did not need to pretend to an ardor or a gratitude she did not feel. Or perhaps it was that she had not been brought up to sensibility and the niceties of courteous behavior.

Certainly her coldness extended beyond himself. Her father had worked hard and schemed hard to net her an aristocratic husband and the life she wanted. And now he was dying, evidently in some pain. And yet she cared not one jot for him. When he had held out his arms to her, she had ignored them and kissed him coldly on the forehead. When he had wanted to celebrate her betrothal, she had told him to go to bed. They might have seemed to be words of kindness and concern, perhaps, if one had not heard the chilly tones in which the words had been uttered.

It was only after he had left the house that he realized that the father had been correct about one thing. She was a beauty. She was of medium height and slim and curved in all the right places. Her hair was a dark red, her eyes green, her mouth wide and generous. Neither the hair nor the mouth seemed to suit the girl's character, though, suggesting as they did warmth and passion.

She was a beauty. He was to have a beautiful countess, if that was any consolation. But he found her totally unappealing. The thought struck him that it was going to take an effort of will to consummate his marriage on his wedding night. Fortunately—if there was anything fortunate about the whole situation—Transome had specified only that there be a consummation and that they inhabit the same house for the first year. He had said nothing about occupying the same bed.

And so the Earl of Falloden resolutely shut his mind to Dorothea Lovestone—small, sweet, feminine Dorothea—and the hurt look there had been in her eyes when he had told her of his betrothal. And he spent every night of the week before his wedding—including the last—with his mistress. Alice had been the one expensive luxury he had allowed himself during the more than a year since he had inherited his title and all the nightmare debts that had come along with it.

She smiled placidly at him as he sat up on the edge of her bed during the early dawn of his wedding day. Alice did everything placidly, including making love. He knew that she did not love him, that she was merely happy to have the security of a regular protector. Perhaps that was what he liked about her. She satisfied his needs without imposing any sort of obligations on him.

"I'll not be coming tonight," he told her, looking

down in distaste at his crumpled clothing, strewn about the floor.

"No, of course not," she said. "This is your wedding day."

Even the announcement of his coming nuptials had not shaken Alice's complacency.

"I'll be here tomorrow night," he said.

"So soon?" She stretched and burrowed farther beneath the blankets. "Will your wife not mind?"

He turned to look at her. Her dark curls were tousled, her eyes sleepy. "Will you mind?" he said. "I'll be here tomorrow, Alice."

"And so will I." She smiled at him. "You are not happy about this marriage, are you, Falloden? You have been very cross all week. But you can always come to me."

The bed looked warm and untidy and inviting. The outline of her body, curled up beneath the blankets, was alluring. He would have liked nothing better at that moment than to join her beneath them once more and spend the day in lovemaking and sleep and forgetfulness.

But it was his wedding day.

He got to his feet, shivered in the chill of the early morning, and reached down for some clothes with which to warm himself.

She was tired. Her maid had clucked her tongue at the paleness of her cheeks and the shadows beneath her eyes and had tried to make up for the fact that she was not in her best looks by curling her hair more elaborately than usual. It was a good thing, she had said, that Miss Ellie was wearing pale blue—and such a lovely simply styled dress with matching cloak—and not a brighter shade to sap even more color from her face.

But she was glad she was tired, Eleanor thought as she walked downstairs to join her father in the parlor. Perhaps she would see her wedding day as if through the haze of drugs. And then she discovered on entering the room that the earl was there already. He was early. And he was magnificent, looking twice as handsome as she remembered him, clad all in shades of blue as if he had known what she was going to wear. He looked as if he were on his way to an audience with the king or Prince Regent. And yet totally unappealing to her. She turned colder at the sight of him and inclined her head unsmilingly. She still refused to curtsy.

And then they were in the carriage and on the way to church and Papa was talking—somehow, through some miracle of willpower, he had succeeded in getting up from his bed that morning despite her protests. The Earl of Falloden was as silent as she.

And then they were at the church and her future husband was introducing another immaculately dressed gentleman—his friend, Sir Albert Hagley. If it were possible to turn colder, she did so as he bowed to her and she inclined her head to him. She recognized him instantly and knew that he recognized her too, though he was far too well bred to say anything, of course. He had been the first to try flirting with her at Pamela Hutchins' country party—if flirting were a strong enough word.

"I am charmed to meet you, ma'am," he said now.

"Good morning, sir," she said.

And then the cold, empty church and the smiling rector. And Papa giving her hand into that of the earl, and the earl's voice repeating the responses dictated by the rector. And her voice doing the same. And then her husband's lips, briefly, motionless, against hers. And the rector's smiles and bows. And Sir Albert's kiss on the cheek and her father's hug, which she could not prevent. And the outdoors again and the earl's carriage.

Her husband's carriage.

Her husband.

They drove to the Earl of Falloden's house on Grosvenor Square—to *her* house. To her new home, where she was bowed to and curtsied to and smiled at by rows of uniformed, liveried servants and led by her husband to the grand dining room, where the wedding breakfast for four was set out. As befitted her new status as Countess of Falloden, she was seated at the foot of the table, opposite her husband. Her father and Sir Albert Hagley sat at either side of the table.

There was conversation. There must have been. She did not afterward remember any awkward silences. But she did not participate in the talk. She could not remember afterward if she ate or not. But finally the meal seemed to be over. Her father got to his feet, a wineglass in his hand, and she began to stretch out a hand to stop him. But she returned it to her lap.

"A toast," he said, beaming around at the other three occupants of the table. "To my beloved daughter and my son-in-law. To the Earl and Countess of Falloden."

Her husband's lips thinned for a moment, she noticed, before relaxing into an arctic smile as his eyes met hers across the length of the table. Sir Albert was on his feet too, repeating the toast and clinking glasses with her father.

Even willpower should not have been enough to have brought Papa from his bed on that day, she thought, looking at him. But it had been. He had scarcely been out of his bed during the past week, and several times he had been delirious. His physician, whom she had summoned two afternoons before, even though he called regularly each morning, had declared that his hours were numbered, that he might go at any time. She had sat up with him for the last three nights, making sure that he had his medicine promptly, straightening his blankets, fluffing his pillows, watching to see that the fire did not burn too low, and snatching sleep in her chair and waking with a start of dread if the room seemed too quiet.

She had begged him not even to try to get up that morning. But he had not only tried but also succeeded. And he had smiled all through the short wedding service and the wedding breakfast. She twisted her hands in her lap and watched him seat himself again and gasp for breath.

"Papa," she said, "you must go home. You must lie down." But her words were stiff and her heart ached in secret. There were two strangers in the room—one of those strangers being her husband.

"I think I will, Ellie," he said, smiling at her in what looked more like a ghastly grimace than a smile.

And fortunately the earl took the hint and got to his feet and sent a servant scurrying to summon her father's carriage.

She wanted to go with him. She *must* go with him. She must stay with him—there was so little time left. And he needed her. She was always the first person he had looked for during the past week on waking up. She had always been the light of his life. He had said it more times than she could remember since the death of her mother when she was five years old. He needed her now.

But he had reminded her that morning that she was to be married, that from that day on she would owe loyalty and obedience to her husband rather than to him. And this was her wedding day and she was in her husband's home. She did not feel close enough to him to ask a favor of him. If there had been an affection between them, if he had been Wilfred, she might have asked permission to return home with her father, wedding day or not. But he was not Wilfred and there was no affection between them.

She could only hope that he would show some sensitivity to the situation and make the suggestion himself. She looked up at him when the two of them moved into the hall to see her father on his way, but she would not beg him, even with her eyes.

"I shall bring your daughter tomorrow to see how you do, sir," he said rather stiffly.

"No hurry, no hurry," her father said, chuckling. "If you two wish to lie abed until noon, I can wait, my lord."

She felt the earl stiffen at the suggestiveness of the words and willed herself not to flush.

"Well," her father said, opening his arms to her. "The Countess of Falloden, Ellie. Perhaps you are too grand a lady now to give your father a hug."

He was so very pleased. So very happy. So very much at the end of his strength. She stepped forward so that the earl would not see her face. But she dared not relax it anyway. Her chest and her throat were raw with the ache of her pain. She kissed him very lightly on the cheek and allowed him to set his arms about her. But she did not put hers about him.

And suddenly that seemed the most cruel part of the whole situation. She wanted to wrap her arms about him and hug him and hug him. She wanted the memory of his aliveness within her arms to carry with her into the days ahead.

"Don't delay any longer, Papa," she said, stepping back. "I shall see you tomorrow."

And she held her chin high and clasped her hands loosely before her, and watched him leave. She felt frozen to the very core. She no longer belonged with him even for the short time that remained to him. She belonged in this strange, large, cold house with the cold stranger who stood at her side. And they had a guest to entertain. Or he had a guest. She did not know if she was expected to play hostess or to withdraw.

"What is your wish?" she asked, turning to look at him and noticing again without any leaping of the heart how very handsome he looked.

"My wish?" He raised his eyebrows. "We will go up to the drawing room, my lady, and you may ring for tea." He extended his arm to her and she took it after a moment's hesitation.

He had delayed long enough, the Earl of Falloden decided, turning determinedly from the window of his bedchamber, through which he had been staring into darkness. He glanced longingly at his bed, neatly turned down for the night, and he thought even more longingly of Alice's wide and soft bed and of Alice's pretty, plump, comfortable body.

There was no point in delaying longer, he thought. He might as well get the deed done since he had no choice in the matter. He could be back and in his own bed for the night in no time at all if he would just make up his mind to go through his dressing room into his wife's and through to her bedchamber.

His wife! The thought appalled him. If he had thought her cold during their first meeting, there was no word frigid enough to describe her as she had been today. Proud and cold and silent, reveling in her new status, only sorry that he was a necessary adjunct to it. And as unfeeling as marble with her father, who was so obviously desperately ill.

He set his hand on the knob of the door connecting their dressing rooms, tapped firmly with his free hand, and turned the knob.

She was not in bed, as he had expected her to be. She was rising from a chair by the fire when he came through from her dressing room. And she stood there straight and proud, looking rather regal, he thought, despite the fact that she was wearing a nightgown and had her hair loose down her back.

The thought that she was beautiful struck him again, quite dispassionately. Her nightgown, all silk and lace—it must have cost Transome a fortune—accentuated the slender curves of her body. And her hair was thick and shiny and wavy, and lay like fire along her back. He thought again of the incongruity of her hair and her character.

"So, my lady," he said, walking toward her across the carpet, "you have become the Countess of Falloden today and gained membership in the *beau monde*. A lifetime's ambition fulfilled?"

There was a half smile on her lips, an expression he had not seen there before. "So, my lord," she said, "you have become debt-free today and rich beyond your wildest dreams. A lifetime's ambition fulfilled?"

He stared at her for a moment, taken aback. *"Tou-*

ché," he said softly at last. "It is a happy day for both of us, it seems."

"Yes." The word was clipped, almost triumphant.

"Except that it is not quite complete yet," he said. "It is not quite a marriage yet."

"No." Her chin moved up a fraction.

"We will proceed to put the final seal on our happiness, then," he said.

"Yes."

Her eyes mocked him. *I have what I want,* they told him. *The rest does not matter.* And righteous indignation was denied him. He had got what he wanted too. Except that he had expected a meek, submissive wife. He felt a surge of anger, and with it the desire to wipe that look from her eyes. The desire to hurt her, to humiliate her. And he was too angry—with himself, perhaps—to be appalled by his desire.

It might all have been over within a very few minutes. He might have laid her down on the bed, raised her nightgown and his nightshirt, and effected a quick consummation. He might have been back in his room within five minutes, a married man in every sense of the word, free to carry on with his life as it had always been except for the inconvenience of having to share his home with his wife for a year.

But he was angry.

He spread one hand behind her neck, pushing his fingers up into her hair, and tilted her head back and sideways. He brought his mouth down on hers open and worked at her lips with his own and with his tongue. He exulted at the immediate stiffening of her body and tightening of her lips, at the way she jerked her head back against his hand, which did not yield one inch. He lifted his head and smiled at her.

"One might almost think that you were made of marble, my lady," he said. And he ignored the voice of decency, very far back in his brain, which reminded him that however objectionable her character, she was in all probability a virgin who had never even been kissed before.

Perhaps he would have relented if she had not chosen to stare steadily back into his eyes and to smile slowly. Except that it was not quite a smile. There was something almost feline about it.

He watched her eyes as he reached out very deliberately to undo the delicate pearl buttons down the front of her nightgown. She lifted her chin even higher when he slid his hands inside to mold her shoulders with his palms and to move them down slowly to cup her breasts. They were warm and silky, firm, not overlarge.

"After all, my lady," he said, nudging at the silk and lace with his wrists so that the gown fell off her shoulders and down her arms, exposing her to the waist, "you are my wife."

It was perhaps at that moment, or a moment later, that anger and the desire to humiliate were changed into desire of a different kind. She took him completely by surprise by reaching up with both hands to undo the large buttons on his nightshirt and very deliberately grasp it by the neck and draw it down over his shoulders.

"After all, my lord," she said, and he noticed her teeth for the first time—white and perfect teeth bared for the moment almost as if she wished to bite into him, "you are my husband."

After that he rather lost his head, he thought later with shame and amazement. He took her hands none too gently by the wrists and forced them downward to her sides so that her nightgown whispered down all the way to the floor and he shrugged out of his own nightshirt, though her hands, when he freed them, pushed at it too. And when he brought his mouth to hers again, her own opened beneath it without persuasion, and when he plunged his tongue inside, she fenced it with her own tongue and followed it out and into his own mouth. And when his hands touched her and explored her without either gentleness or subtlety, her own hands followed suit.

One thing at least must have been as clear to her as

it was to him before he finally stooped down to pick her up and half throw her onto the bed. He was going to have no trouble at all feeling enough desire for her to enable him to consummate their marriage.

She wrestled with him on the bed, so that by the time he had her pinned beneath him they were both panting. He worked his knees between her thighs, pushed them wide, slid his hands beneath her, and lifted his head. She was staring boldly up at him, her cheeks flushed, her hair wild about her shoulders and over the pillow. He found the entrance to her and came inside her with one deep, swift thrust.

Her expression did not change. Only her body tensed and tried to pull back away from his penetration. For a few moments. But as he watched, she half smiled again and slid her feet up on the bed on either side of his legs to brace herself and very deliberately pushed down against him.

"Almost my wife, my lady," he whispered to her. "The deed is almost done."

"I thought it was to hurt," she said. "I thought it was to be something earth-shattering."

He might even then, his triumph complete, her body spread and mounted beneath him, have had some small mercy on her and finished quickly. But she had restored his anger by her foolish attack on his manhood. She would be made to know, then, what it was to be duty bound to cater to his pleasure, what it meant to be obliged to grant him his conjugal rights. He would make all her future days ones of anxiety, wondering if she must face this again when the night came.

He began to move in her, watching her face. She looked back, but something far back in her eyes assured him that she had not known of this, that she had thought the one penetration of her body all that was to be endured. He set up a slow rhythm before finally lowering his weight off his elbows and onto her warm feminine curves and continuing, making sure that he withdrew almost completely from her with each downward movement and reached deeply into her with each upward one. And he listened to the wetness of their coupling and the rhythmic creaking of the bedsprings and her ragged breathing and his own, imposing the last ounce of control over himself so that he would not climax before he was quite ready to do so.

But it was not easy. He gradually became aware over the thudding of his heart and the surging of his blood that her legs had hooked themselves around his and her pelvis tilted to allow an even deeper penetration. And inner muscles were drawing on him, resisting his withdrawals and relaxing around his entries. And her hips were swaying against his.

He grasped her shoulders, slid his hands down her back to grasp her buttocks and still her movements, and pushed urgently and mindlessly up into her depths until a blessed shattering brought his release. He heard a shout and rather thought that it must have been his voice.

She was shuddering violently beneath him. He held his weight firmly on her until she gradually relaxed. And perhaps for longer than that. He had the distinct impression when he finally thought of moving off her that he was just waking up from sleep. But the candles were still bright, and the fire still burned in the grate.

He lay beside her, looking at her. Neither of them had pulled up the blankets. Her dark red hair lay in wild disarray all about her, making her pale breasts look as if they might be made of alabaster. At least now, he thought, the red hair did not seem quite so out of place. She had an earthy, passionate nature that he had not dreamt it possible for a woman to possess. Least of all this woman. Perhaps it came from her less than noble background, though in his experience even mistresses and whores exercised more decorum in the bedchamber than she. Passionate nature and cold, cold heart.

"Well," he said, "the deed is thoroughly done. At least I will never now be able to annul our marriage, my lady, and deprive you of your precious title."

"And at least," she said, "I will never be able to have our marriage annulled, my lord, and deprive you of your precious fortune."

"*Touché* once more," he said. "Well, the happiest day of our lives is over, my lady, much to our mutual regret, I am sure. I shall leave you to dream of the triumph of your new status while I return to my own bed to dream of counting piles of gold. Good night."

He looked down at her as he got to his feet. The sheet and her inner thighs were a mess of blood. But she did not even try to cover herself. She looked up at him with that half smile he found so unpleasant.

"Good night," she said. "I doubt the night will be long enough to count every pile, my lord. My father is very, very wealthy."

"I know," he said, bending to retrieve his nightshirt but not stopping to pull it on before leaving her room.

He glanced at a clock in his dressing room. More than an hour had passed since he had entered his wife's room. A wave of revulsion set him to shivering as he poured water that was almost cold into the basin on the washstand and proceeded to wash himself. Revulsion against the strange cold, passionate woman he had married. And revulsion against himself for indulging hatred and animal instincts he had not known himself capable of.

At least, he thought, it was all over now. Both this house and Grenfell Park were large enough that they could avoid each other for most of their days. And after a year had passed he could make sure that she was always in a house where he was not. And if he should ever feel the need for an heir of his own body—well, he would think of that when the time came. He was only twenty-eight years old.

She had bled a great deal more than he would have expected a virgin to bleed, he thought, looking at the distinctly pink hue of the water. And he felt shame for his roughness, and hatred against her for having provoked it.

He could scarcely wait for the following night, he thought, closing his eyes and reaching for his night-shirt. Tomorrow night and the comfortable sanity of Alice's bed and body.

bed from the dressing room. But she must have done
so because that was where she was now lying. And
she was wearing her nightgown, she noticed, feeling
it with one hand. She could not remember pulling it

4

She woke up feeling the strangeness of her surround-
ings—the large square, high-ceilinged room, the bed,
wider and softer than her own, its elaborate hangings
green instead of rose pink. She realized what had
woken her when she spotted a maid, on her knees,
quietly building up the fire. Someone else was in her
dressing room. There was a clinking of china. It was
probably a pitcher of hot water being set down.

And then came the feeling of surprise that she had
slept at all. She had not expected to. And yet she could
remember standing in her dressing room, washing herself off with hands that shook from fear and shock.
She remembered leaning on her forearms on the washstand and closing her eyes and contemplating the full
horror of what had just happened—of what he had done
to her and of the way she had reacted. She had done
what she always did when she was afraid or angry or
both. She had given as good as she had got. She had
fought her fear—literally fought. She had never been
so terrified as she had been when her husband came
to her. She had never fought such a desperate fight.

And yet she could remember yawning despite everything. Yawning and yawning and wondering how she was
to get herself back from the dressing room to the bed.
She had had three almost sleepless nights and she had
lived through an hour of terror and an hour of frightening abandon, at some time during which she lost
herself completely, so that she had somehow woken as
if from sleep to find herself pinned beneath his full
weight. She could not now remember returning to her

bed from the dressing room. But she must have done so because that was where she was now lying. And she was wearing her nightgown, she noticed, feeling it with one hand. She could not remember pulling it back on.

One of the hardest things she had done in her life, she found half an hour later, was dismissing her maid and leaving her dressing room to descend to the breakfast room. She dreaded seeing him again—the stiff and contemptuous stranger who had so hurt and degraded her the night before. Her husband. She drew back her shoulders and raised her head high.

But the breakfast room was empty except for the butler and a footman and rows of silver-covered warming dishes on a sideboard.

"Good morning, m'lady," the butler said, bowing deeply and drawing back a chair for her.

And that was what she was, she thought with some incredulity. She was my lady, a countess. The Countess of Falloden. The thought made her heart sink lower than it already was.

"Good morning, Mr. Starret," she said, smiling at him as she always smiled at her father's servants. "Good morning." She looked at the footman. "I do not know your name."

"Peter, my lady," he said, seeming startled and jumping to attention. "Good morning, my lady."

"Good morning, Peter," she said.

The butler had a message for her. His lordship would be ready to escort her to her father's house as soon as she had breakfasted. The words brought on a wave of nausea and she asked only for a slice of toast. He was going to come with her, then, as he had told Papa the day before that he would. She was not going to be able to escape from him. And Papa. She realized with a jolt of surprise and shame that she had not thought of him all night or even when she had got up. How could she not have thought of him? How could she have slept?

She felt a wave of panic. Had he lived through the

night? Would they arrive home only to find that he was already gone? What would she do? She would not be able to face the aloneness with Papa gone. Especially now. And yet the selfishness of the thought filled her with new shame. She set her napkin beside her plate and the half-eaten slice of toast, and the butler rushed forward to draw back her chair.

"Thank you, Mr. Starret," she said. "Will you inform my husband that I will be ready to leave in five minutes' time?" She had to use all her willpower not to rush from the room.

She was the marble lady again, seated silent and straight-backed beside him in his carriage, watching the world go by outside her window. He watched her as they rode through the streets of London. She looked startlingly lovely in rich brown velvet, a color that might have looked drab on any other woman. But it suited her hair. She sat stiff and proud. She might have been a duchess, he thought, and guessed that she must have rehearsed her triumphal entry into the ranks of the *ton* with great care. No one would realize, seeing her this morning, that she was nothing but a cit's daughter.

And his countess. He remembered the night before with renewed shame. He had never handled even a whore with such roughness as he had used on his wife. He might have apologized to her. In fact, he had rehearsed an apology when waiting in the library while she got up and had breakfast. And yet she had looked at him with such cool disdain when she joined him in the hall, ready to leave, and had bidden him good morning with such cold haughtiness, that his apology had faded from his lips and his mind. He had bowed and returned her greeting.

The only words they had exchanged that morning. And yet, he remembered in amazement, she had been like a tigress the night before. A tigress in heat. It was difficult to reconcile that memory of her with the very real image of the ice goddess seated beside him. He unclothed her with his eyes but could not quite see the same woman with whom he had been naked and wildly intimate a mere matter of hours before.

"I thank you for your escort, my lord," she said as they approached her father's house. She did not turn to look at him. "But there is no need for you to descend. I shall return to Grosvenor Square later in my father's carriage."

"On the contrary, my lady," he said, "I shall pay your father the courtesy of a personal call."

He vaulted out of the carriage ahead of her and handed her down. Straw had been strewn about in a thick layer on the pavement and roadway in front of the house, he saw, and yards of cloth had been wound about the brass knocker. He was thankful for the moment that his wife was cold and insensitive and reacted to these signs of desperate illness and imminent death within the house just as if she did not see them.

Mr. Transome was upstairs in bed with his physician in attendance, the servant who opened the door explained in answer to the earl's question—his wife stood silent at his side. And yes, his lordship could indeed wait upon the master. Mr. Transome had requested it.

They waited until the physician came downstairs. She led the way into the parlor and stood facing the fire, warming her hands. He might have moved up behind her and set his hands on her shoulders and offered some word of comfort. But she looked unconcerned. Would not any normal daughter have bounded up the stairs two at a time, physician or no physician?

The physician was shown into the parlor as the earl had requested and bowed obsequiously and shifted his weight from foot to foot with embarrassment. Mr. Transome was gravely ill. Miss Transome—her ladyship, that is—must prepare herself for his demise at any moment. The doctor had left instructions for the medication to be doubled in dosage, but Mr. Transome had refused to take more than his usual amount before speaking first with his lordship and her ladyship. The doctor finally bowed himself out.

The earl, for good reason, felt no great affection for his father-in-law. Nevertheless, he looked in anger at his wife's back. She had not once turned from the fire while the physician was in the room.

"I shall wait upon your father now, my lady," he said. "You may stay here until I come down. I shall not be long."

She said nothing.

The difference in the appearance of his father-in-law was appalling. The earl realized in a flash just what superhuman effort of will had brought the man to Grosvenor Square on two separate occasions the week before and to his daughter's wedding just the day before. Now he was very obviously a man close to death. And yet he managed the ghost of a smile when the earl came to stand beside his bed.

"Ah, my lord," he said in a voice that was little above a whisper, "you will excuse me for not rising to make my bow."

"How are you, sir?" the earl asked, feeling all the foolishness of his words.

"I have felt better," Mr. Transome said, and even attempted a chuckle. "So what do you have to tell me?"

"Your daughter is my wife and my countess in every sense," the earl said.

"Ah." Mr. Transome closed his eyes. "I wish I could see my first grandchild, my lord. But I must not be greedy."

The earl looked down at him, his hands clasped behind his back.

"Where is Ellie?" Mr. Transome asked.

"Downstairs," the earl said, "and impatient to be with you, sir. But I thought you might wish to have a private word with me first."

"There is a small parcel and a letter in the top drawer of the bureau," Mr. Transome said. "Fetch them. And here am I giving orders to you, my lord. You must forgive me. You are my son now, after all."

The earl found the two items with ease. The top

drawer of the bureau was empty except for them. He brought them back to the bed and showed them to the man lying there.

"A Christmas present for Ellie," Mr. Transome said with the hint of a smile. "I had it made on the chance that I would live that long and yet be too ill to go shopping. I could give it to her now and watch her face when she saw it, but it is better kept for Christmas. Give it to her, my lord. And the letter to explain a few things."

"It will be done," the earl said.

"Ah." Mr. Transome closed his eyes again. "I shall be saying good-bye then, my boy. Forgive me for the trick I played on you. Eventually you will thank me, I believe, but for now forgive me. She is all that has made my life worth living since her dear mother passed on."

"She is in safe hands," the earl said, feeling a twinge of guilt at the lie, his mind filling unwillingly with memories of the night before. "On that point you may rest assured. Good-bye, sir."

He let himself out of the room and stood still outside the door for a moment before descending to the parlor. And yes, he thought, he almost could forgive the man. He had made arrangements for his daughter's future security in the only way he knew how—by using his money to buy what he wanted. And who could blame him?

The only pity was that all the love and work and scheming had been expended on such an unworthy object. The earl gritted his teeth and turned toward the staircase.

She stood staring into the fire. He was dying. She had known that. She might expect his demise at any time, the doctor had said. She had known that too. But all the horrible reality of it had come home to her when the horses' hooves and the carriage wheels had suddenly become muffled and when she had stepped down from the carriage onto straw and looked up to see the knocker wrapped with cloth. It had come home to her then in all its harsh truth.

And it had been her husband, not she, who had asked for news, who had directed that the doctor be shown into the parlor as soon as he came downstairs, who had questioned him when he came. It was her husband who had gone up first to Papa, not she.

She had been paralyzed by the new knowledge that was not new at all. The full stark realization that her father was dying, that soon she would be left alone. Alone with a cold and frightening stranger who had not spoken even a single word of sympathy during their wait for the doctor. Not that she sought or wanted sympathy from him. But—oh, yes, she did. She wanted a kind voice and kind hands—anyone's, even his.

The door opened behind her.

"You may go up, my lady," he said. "He is waiting for you."

How is he? she almost asked. Foolish, fruitless words. She turned from the fire. "I will stay with him," she said, looking him directly in the eye, "until he is dead. With your permission, my lord."

He nodded. "I shall return later," he said, "to see how he goes on."

She was still wearing her cloak and bonnet, she realized suddenly. She removed them and set them down on a chair, folding her cloak carefully. She dreaded going up. She knew that after yesterday he would have finally given in to his inevitable end. She knew he would be very close to death. She wanted someone to go with her. She wanted an arm to lean on.

"Do you want me to come up with you?" he asked.

"No, thank you," she said, looking at him coolly and sweeping past him in the doorway and up the stairs. She felt like two quite separate people, she thought, the one who thought and felt and the one who spoke and acted. She was frightened by the thought that she could not be sure which was the real Eleanor Transome-Eleanor Pierce.

Her father sounded as if he were snoring. But when

she tiptoed to his bedside and nodded to the house-keeper to indicate that she could leave, she found that he was awake.

"Papa?" she said.

"Ellie." She knew he was smiling even though his face did not quite register the expression. "My own little countess."

"Yes," she said, bending to kiss his forehead very lightly.

"Is he treating you well, Ellie?" he asked.

"Yes, Papa," she lied. "He is very kind."

"And gentle, Ellie?"

"And gentle," she said, remembering the searing pain.

"Forgive me, Ellie," he said. "I know this is not what you wanted. But I know more of life than you. I believe you will be happy. Forgive me?"

"Papa," she said.

"I loved your mama," he said. "And you were born of her, Ellie—more precious than anyone or anything else in my life."

"Papa," she said, "don't talk anymore." His words had been interspersed with loud rasping breaths.

He obeyed her for a while. He lay still with closed eyes, looking and sounding again as if he were asleep. But he opened his eyes eventually.

"Promise me something, Ellie," he said.

"Anything, Papa." She leaned closer.

"Don't mourn long for me," he said. "I know you love me, girl. You don't need to show it to the world with black clothes and gloom. You are a new bride, Ellie, and will be a new mother before the first year is out, I have no doubt. And Christmas is coming. Promise me you will put off your mourning before Christmas and have a wonderful celebration. Have Christmas for me. It was always my favorite time of year. Promise me."

"Oh, Papa," she said.

"Promise." He reached out one bony hand and grabbed feebly for her wrist.

"I promise," she said. "We will have a warm and wonderful Christmas, Papa."

"Ah," he said.

They were the last coherent words he spoke. When he grew restless a short while later, she fetched him his medicine and gave him twice the usual dose. And she sat beside his bed, her hands in her lap, not touching either him or the bed, afraid of causing him more pain. She watched him sink into a deep stupor, which gradually lightened as the hours passed until it was time for a renewal of the medicine.

And soon a pattern was established, the hours of relative calm interspersed with intervals of tossing and turning and muttering. He mentioned her name many times and her mother's name. Eventually he called her name no more but only her mother's and once her grandmother's and her grandfather's.

She had no idea how long it lasted. She did know that several times she refused to be persuaded to go to bed for a rest and that once she allowed herself to be persuaded to eat, though the tray went back almost as full as it had been when it arrived. She was only half aware that the doctor and the housekeeper and other servants came and went from the room. She only half heard the housekeeper tell her on three separate occasions that his lordship had called.

She neither knew nor cared if it was hours or days or weeks that passed. It was actually the evening of the day following her arrival. His breathing had changed. There were longer intervals between the loud raspings.

"He is going, poor dear soul," the housekeeper whispered.

But she did not hear the words. She held his hand very lightly in hers and knew from his mumblings earlier that she was already superfluous to him, being still anchored firmly in the land of the living. She knew that he was seeing only her mother and his own parents. She knew that he had already gone from her, that he needed now to shed the nuisance of a body that would no longer serve him.

She felt only her own loss. He was beyond pain or fear.

"He is gone, my lady. I am so sorry, my lady." The soft voice and the hands on her shoulders were those of the housekeeper.

And she realized that there were no more breaths at all. She sat and held his hand for a while longer before laying it down gently at his side so as not to cause him pain. And she leaned forward and kissed it.

"Good-bye, Papa," she said.

"His lordship is downstairs, my lady," the housekeeper said. "You go to him. I'll see to everything here."

"Thank you." Eleanor got to her feet and straightened her shoulders. "Thank you, Mrs. Bennet." She did not look at her father again.

"He is dead," she said. "He died a few minutes ago."

"I am so sorry," he said, and he took a step toward her. She was still wearing the brown velvet dress she had put on the morning of the day before. Her hair looked as if it had not been combed since. Her face was pale, her eyes dark-shadowed. He would have gone to her, perhaps even drawn her into his arms. He had been impressed to learn on each of his visits that she could not be persuaded to leave the sickroom. Perhaps he had misjudged her.

"There is no need to be," she said. "He should have died a month ago. Only stubbornness kept him alive so long."

He stood still and watched her. "Come and sit down," he said.

"It was kind of you to call so frequently," she said. "I thank you." She did not move from her standing position just inside the door.

"He was my father-in-law," he said. "And you are my wife."

Incredibly, she smiled. "What a lowering admission for you to have to make," she said.

"My carriage is outside," he said. "I shall send you home in it, my lady, with a maid. You need sleep. I shall stay to see the physician when he arrives and to begin making arrangements for . . . To begin making arrangements."

"For the funeral," she said. "Yes. Thank you. It is kind of you to be willing to do that. I shall return tomorrow morning—with your permission. There will be letters to write, people to inform."

Even then he considered going to her. What would happen if he took her by the shoulders? Would she relax her proud posture, set her head against him, and allow the floodgates of grief to be opened? *Was* there grief? Or would she continue to stand stiffly, perhaps, and look at him in incomprehension and even with contempt?

"Are you all right?" he asked her.

"All right?" Her eyes widened. "I am tired. He was a long time going. Far longer than I expected."

He remained where he was. "On your way, then," he said, "without further delay."

She stared at him silently for a long moment and then turned and left the room without another word.

He stood looking after her. Would she have behaved differently if he had been someone else? he wondered. Could she possibly be as cold and unfeeling as she seemed? Was it hatred of him that caused her to hold her feelings in check? Or were there no feelings?

It chilled him to know that he was married to such a woman. And to know that his marriage weighed more heavily on his mind than he had expected it to do. He had done nothing in the past two days except move between his own house and Transome's. There had been no visits to White's or any of the other clubs. And it was not until this very moment that he remembered telling Alice that he would be with her the night before. His spirits had been oppressed by the dying of a man who was a stranger to him. A stranger he had good reason to dislike. And by the girl who was losing a father and who had every reason to believe that she was being transferred to the care of a man who would treat her far more cruelly.

It shamed him to know that he was that man. And yet how could he show kindness to a marble statue? To a woman who was a social climber and nothing else? How could he be kind to a woman who hated him? A woman who spoke of her father's death as if it meant nothing at all to her, as if spending his last hours with him had been nothing but an exhausting nuisance to her?

And did he want to show kindness to her anyway? She was the daughter of a cit. He had been forced into marrying her. And he would always feel some shame, knowing that he had agreed to the marriage for the sake of money. He had never thought of himself as a mercenary man.

But it was not the time for such thoughts, he realized suddenly. There were things to be done. Although it was already late evening, there was a man upstairs who had just died, and doubtless the servants would be seeking direction on what to do. He drew a deep breath and opened the door into the hallway.

She held herself stiff and her mind blank until she was finally alone in her bedchamber on Grosvenor Square. She had waved away her maid and undressed herself. She sank into the chair where she had waited for her husband to come to her on their wedding night—how many nights ago? She did not know. And she prepared to cry her heart out.

She stared into the crackling flames of the fire and thought of her father. Thought of the way she had been the focus of his life all through her childhood and girl-hood, although he had always worked long hours. Thought of how he had always lavished love and gifts on her. And of how her world had revolved about him. Thought of him sick and in pain for the last months, though he had never complained and had refused to let his brothers and sisters know how gravely ill he was and had forbidden her to inform them. They had their own lives and worries, he said, and did not need to be burdened with his. She thought of him dying, slowly fading from her and from life through the long hours when she had sat by his side. Thought of his still, quiet body when she had finally released his hand and turned from him.

She thought of the fact that she would never see him again. He was gone from her. Forever, just as her mother had been abruptly and permanently gone from her childhood. She was alone. Her father was dead. The dearest person in all the world to her, including Wilfred—oh, yes, even including him—was dead.

And she waited for the tears, for the release of grief and the relief from the unbearable pain of loss. But there was only the pain, the pain of knowing at last that she could not grieve. She was too tired to grieve. She had never in her life felt more tired.

If only he had been someone else when she had gone downstairs to the parlor. If only he had been one of her uncles or cousins. She felt sorry again that Papa had chosen not to inform his family of the gravity of his illness. They would have come—Papa's family always rallied around for a big occasion, even if that occasion was an illness and death.

If he had been one of her uncles, she could have walked straight into his arms and buried her face against his chest and howled out her loss. She could have done it then. She had needed to do it then. But he was an aristocrat and cold to the very heart. Had she gone to him, he would probably have been more concerned about her tears taking the starch from his neckcloth than about her distress. He would have looked down at her with disdain and contempt. Doubtless in his world it was not considered good *ton* to weep for a dead father.

Besides, she would not put her feelings on display for him. She would not.

Papa! Eleanor spread weary hands over her face and

longed for the relief of tears. And longed for someone to go to, for someone's arms and someone's shoulder and someone's soothing voice. But when she thought of her husband again, she could remember only what he had done to her in this very room a few nights before.

She could not cry. She gave up even trying after a while and moved over to the bed and lay down on it after blowing out the candles. But she could not sleep either. She was more tired than she could ever remember being, but she could not sleep.

She stared into the fire and wondered what he was doing. And wondered if he would come home at all that night.

5

Old habits died hard, he supposed. She came back to her father's house quite early on the morning after his death, fully intending to write letters there to her relatives. And yet when he told her that she might write them at home—in Grosvenor Square—she made no objection. She merely looked blankly at him and agreed to return with him in the carriage. She looked about her almost as if she were in a strange house.

He had had a sleepless night, and she too looked unrefreshed even though he had sent her home to bed. Her face was pale and lifeless and her eyes darkshadowed. He wondered, as he had done the evening before, what she would do if he moved closer to her and set a hand on her shoulder or about her shoulders, perhaps. Would she respond to the gesture of sympathy? It was hard to tell. He did not know if her calm was the result of a monumental self-control or if it was a part of her nature. And yet he could find no evidence that there were feelings beneath the calm and the apparent coldness.

"Your father has been washed and laid out," he told her gently. "He is still in his bed. Do you wish to see him?"

She thought for a moment. "No," she said.

Perhaps she was afraid. Afraid of death. "Will it help if I come with you?" he asked.

She turned her eyes on him. "Not at all," she said. "Thank you."

"I shall have a dressmaker summoned to the house," he told her when they were in the carriage.

"It will save you the distress of having to go out. She can make up all the mourning clothes you will need. Do you have a preference for any particular modiste?"

"No," she said. "And I will not need much. Only a few dresses for the next few weeks. I will leave off my mourning before Christmas. And you must too—if you intend to wear mourning at all, my lord. I do not imagine you felt any great fondness for my father."

"Leave off mourning before Christmas?" he said, appalled. "After only a month?" He ignored her final words.

"Why wear black for longer?" she asked. "As a show for the world? I do not care to impress the world."

"I believe you care very much, my lady," he said. "Or why was it so important to you to marry a titled man? One can hardly say, after all, that you married me for my money."

"Or for love," she said. "Perhaps I married you for your good looks, my lord. I am sure you must know that you have those in abundance."

"This is hardly the time or place in which to quarrel," he said, frowning. "I am afraid that I must insist that you wear mourning clothes for at least a year, my lady. I have respect for the dead if you do not."

"It was his request," she said, looking at him disdainfully. "His final request, my lord. That I not mourn for him long. That I put off mourning before Christmas. But of course, I owe obedience to you now, do I not? No longer to a father who is not even alive."

There was bitterness in her tone. And what further proof did he need that she cared not a jot for anyone but herself? He did not believe her. But how could he take the chance of not doing so? Would she forever hold against him the fact that he had not allowed her to honor her father's last request?

"Very well, then," he said curtly. "But you will not be seen in public within the next year, my lady. Not in town, anyway. We will remove to the country—

to Grenfell Park—and stay there. I am sorry you will
have no Season next spring. I am sure you have your
heart set upon it." And she would too, he thought in
cold anger. She would dance and make merry within
months of her father's death if he would allow it.

"Ah," she said, "but I will have Grenfell Park, my
lord, and all the glory of being its mistress. I will take
precedence over everyone else, will I not? Do you have
a padded pew at church? I shall enjoy walking down
the aisle, nodding condescendingly to all our neighbors."

"You have a wicked tongue," he said. "Will any of
your family be present for the funeral, do you suppose?"

"No," she said. "Most of my father's family live
in or close to Bristol. There will not be time for letters
to reach them and the journey to London to be made.
You may relax, my lord. You are not about to be surrounded by hordes of vulgar business people and farmers. Just me and my father's business associates from
town. I am sure that that will be agony and humiliation
enough."

He considered retreating into silence since they were
quite close to home anyway. But he must begin as he
meant to proceed, he decided. He did not intend to
take cover in silence from the barbed tongue of a
shrew.

"I think we had better decide, my lady," he said,
looking directly at her, his voice stern, "to treat each
other with courtesy. It seems that we both entered this
marriage for less than admirable reasons, and it has
become clear that neither of us feels even the smallest
degree of affection for the other. But married we are,
and married we will remain for the rest of our lives.
Let there be civility between us, then. And civility of
manner as well as word. No more sarcasm and biting
setdowns."

The hostility gradually faded from her eyes as he
watched her, to be replaced by wariness. "Very well,"
she said at last.

But any chance he might have had of comforting her for the death of her father—if she needed comforting—was lost. He handed her from the carriage when they arrived at Grosvenor Square and she disappeared into the morning room to write her letters while he retired to his own room to sleep for a few hours. And yet he found himself overtired. He could not sleep.

And he found himself wishing he could live the last few days over again. He wished that he had followed his own recent advice and established a relationship of mutual respect from the start between himself and his wife. He wished he could have his wedding night over again. He wished he could consummate his marriage with more gentleness and consideration. But perhaps things could not have been different anyway. Perhaps his wife was as cold and as shrewish as she had seemed so far in his acquaintance with her.

And yet she was unexpectedly hot in some ways. He closed his eyes and remembered the wildness and the boldness with which she had made love to him. He would have sworn that she had had a great deal of experience if it had not been for the blood—and for the barrier that he had felt himself tearing through. And he remembered the frenzy with which he had finally ended that encounter, shouting out, spilling his seed into her with all control gone.

He inhaled slowly. It had not been the way he liked it—not that he had had it like that before. He liked sanity and warm comfort between the sheets with his women. And yet, he realized with no small annoyance as he turned onto his side and tried to will himself to sleep, he was aroused. Just thinking of his wedding night had aroused him.

What he had said in the carriage on the way home the morning after her father's death, Eleanor decided over the coming days and weeks, was sensible, and she was glad that it had been said even though his voice and his eyes had been icy when he spoke and she had been chilled by the knowledge that she owed this man obedience for the rest of her life.

But she was glad afterward that he had spoken thus. The following days would have been difficult under any circumstances, but they would have been a great deal worse if he had not put a stop to the open hostility between them. For she saw a great deal more of him during the day then she had ever seen of her father.

Mostly it was unavoidable. The *ton* arrived in force during the five days preceding the funeral, and even afterward, to meet the bride of the Earl of Falloden, to congratulate them both on their marriage, to sympathize with them on their bereavement. Mostly they came out of curiosity, she thought, to see the cit's daughter who had netted one of their own most eligible matrimonial catches. To look at her and criticize every detail of her appearance and behavior. To look for signs of vulgarity.

And she would have given them what they wanted, she sometimes thought—as she had at Pamela's party two years before—if she had not made that agreement with her husband and if he had not stayed so unwaveringly at her side through all the visits. Perhaps he stayed close just to prevent the sort of situation that would case him embarrassment. But whatever his reason, he was always there beside her, his hand sometimes resting at her waist as he presented her to numerous strangers as his wife.

He stayed at her side even when her father's friends and associates came to express their sympathies, as several did. And he conversed courteously with them, even with Mr. Simms with his broad cockney accent, keeping his bargain with her as she kept hers with him.

It was strangely comforting—except when she thought about the reality of the situation, as she did occasionally in the privacy of her own room. It was all a facade, a mere matter of civility, a way of getting through life without the unpleasantness of confrontation. It was fine for the days leading up to the funeral and for the weeks following it. But she found herself waiting for life to get back to normal again, waiting to go home. She was finding it almost impossible to accept the fact that this was now normal life, that this was home. That her father was no more. That the Earl of Falloden was the man with whom she must spend the rest of her life. Randolph. She could not quite associate the name with him. Or any other name, for that matter. He was the Earl of Falloden to her.

There was not even the smallest degree of affection between them, he had said. His words were perfectly true. There was not. And yet the reality of it frightened her. She had grown up with deep affection—with her father and with the other members of her family when they were together as they quite often were. But her father was dead, and her family was lost to her. Her husband would not wish to lower himself to associating with them. Was she to live the rest of her life without affection, then? She already felt starved after a few weeks. Ravenously hungry for love.

And angry and dreadfully upset when Wilfred responded to the letter she had written to his father with a passionate love letter. All the love that might feed her aching and empty heart. Yet a forbidden love.

Perhaps, she thought at first, if she could just be patient, she would within a year or so have a child on whom to lavish all the pent-up love that was fairly bursting from her. Even though it would be his child, it would be hers too, and a person in its own right. But hope even for that faded as the days and then the weeks passed and he never came to her at night. For which blessing she was profoundly thankful. She found herself almost sick with dread for the first couple of weeks when she retired to bed. But without those terrifying encounters there would be no child.

She did not know how she would live with an empty, meaningless marriage, and with no children. Being an only child herself, she had always dreamed of having a large family of her own—five or six children. And dogs and cats. And—oh, and life and love and laughter.

For the first two weeks after the funeral she at least had the evenings to herself. After dinner, during which they always conversed politely on impersonal topics, she retired to her sitting room while he did she knew not what. She did not even know whether he went out or stayed at home. He never entered her sitting room, which was at the opposite side of her bedchamber from her dressing room. And so she made of the room her own private domain, rearranging the furniture for maximum coziness, filling it with her own personal belongings from home—from her father's home after she had spent a day there gathering together what she wished to keep. And in her private sitting room she read and sewed and felt almost happy.

But that was not to last.

"What do you do in the evenings?" he asked her abruptly one day at dinner.

"I read," she said. "Or I embroider. Or I knit. All those things that any real lady does, my lord." But she flushed under his steady gaze. She did not often forget their agreement. "I am sorry."

"Bring your book or your embroidery or whatever you choose to do this evening to the library, then," he said. "We might as well spend our evenings in a room together since we seem on the whole to have learned to be civil to each other."

"Yes, my lord," she said. But she felt only dismay and a sinking of the heart at having to obey this man's every whim. Life was not fair to women, she thought. And that was an understatement. She wondered what he would say or do if she refused or at least expressed her reluctance to obey. And yet, looking at him as he signaled a footman to refill his wineglass, she reminded herself that he was at least human, that at least spending the evening in the same room with him would give the illusion of closeness, would take away some of the loneliness of her existence.

She fetched her embroidery to the library, knowing that it would be pointless to bring a book, knowing that she would not be able to concentrate on its pages.

And she settled herself into a deep leather chair on one side of the roaring fire while he sat at the other, a book spread on his lap. And she bent her head over her work and found that she had been wrong. There was an aching loneliness, far worse than that she felt usually of an evening. For it was a cozy room and warm against the early December chill. And her husband was sprawled comfortably in his chair. It was the perfect domestic scene.

And yet it was all illusion. They were strangers, unhappy strangers, who had agreed for the sake of good sense to live together with civility. There was no affection, no closeness whatsoever. She could not, if she wished to do so, lift her head to share some confidence or some piece of nonsense with him.

She lifted her head to look at him. He was looking steadily at her, his book neglected on his lap.

"It is pretty," he said, indicating the cloth on which she worked.

"Thank you." She lowered her head again.

"I have four fellows coming to Grenfell Park for Christmas," he said. "I had invited them out there before our wedding for a few days of shooting. Do you wish me to put them off? It would be easy to do, what with my sudden marriage and your bereavement."

Four gentlemen. To be entertained over Christmas. She turned cold. And one of them would doubtless be Sir Albert Hagley.

"No," she said. "It would not be right, my lord."

"Is there anyone that you would like to invite, then?" he asked. "Some friend or friends? You have not associated with any since our marriage, but there must be some. Are there?"

"There is no one of your class, my lord," she said. "No one with whom your four friends would be pleased to mingle."

"Invite them anyway," he said. "I will leave it to your discretion, my lady, to invite only those who will feel comfortable."

They were fair words, she thought. Civil. And yet

looked at another way, they were insufferably condescending. She could invite some friends provided they
did not murder the English language every time they
opened their mouths? Or laughed too loudly at a joke?
Or dipped their fingers into the gravy?

"Thank you," she said. "How many do you wish
me to invite?"

"As many as you like," he said.

She bent her head over her work again, and he said
no more. She was busily trying to decide whom she
would invite. But her friends would be reluctant to
leave their families over Christmas. She would invite
some people, however. She would think of someone.
She remembered suddenly her promise to her father to
make Christmas a warm and wonderful celebration.
She could hardly do that if she were alone with five
gentlemen.

Yes, she would find someone—or preferably a few
people—to invite. And if her husband's four friends
did not like mingling with cits and other members of
the middle class, well, then, she would treat them accordingly. After all, her promise to be civil had strictly
speaking been made only to her husband in her dealings with him.

She looked up at him, prepared to do battle if he
should have anything else condescending to say. But
he was reading his book and looked deeply absorbed
in it.

By the next day Eleanor had decided that she would
invite two aunts, her father's sisters, and the two unmarried daughters of one of them to spend Christmas
at Grenfell Park. Aunt Beryl had been married to a
tenant farmer until his death five years before. He had
worked hard and left Aunt Beryl and Muriel and Mabel in comfortable circumstances. Aunt Ruth had always lived with them. She had never married.

They were refined, she thought. Indeed, they had
several times dined with Lord Sharples, whose tenants
they had been. Aunt Beryl boasted frequently about

those occasions. But Eleanor despised herself for choosing the most refined of her relatives to invite. As if it mattered. As if she cared what her husband or his four gentlemen friends would think. She loved all her relatives. The times when they came together for various celebrations had always been the highlights of her life.

She would have written the invitations during the morning, but the housekeeper suggested that they go over the household accounts together. Her husband was from home and would be gone for most of the day, he had told her at breakfast. He was closing her father's affairs with her father's man of business.

And she would have written during the afternoon, but visitors called again. There were not many any longer, but most days brought one or two. Mr. Simms came, bringing with him his wife, who had been ill the first time he came. Mrs. Simms looked about her in awe, although her husband was almost as wealthy as Papa had been. But she relaxed and settled for a comfortable coze when she knew that his lordship was from home. She and Mr. Simms rose to leave only when Lady Lovestone and her daughter arrived. Eleanor had not met them before.

They were so sorry not to have paid a call earlier, Lady Lovestone assured Lady Falloden, but . . . There was a string of excuses. Eleanor smiled at her and at her pretty blond daughter, who sat silently staring at her.

"I was never more surprised in my life," Lady Lovestone said, "than when I heard of Falloden's betrothal and hasty marriage. Of course, he was living under difficult circumstances, poor man. And your father was a . . . ?"

"Mr. Joseph Transome," Eleanor said. But her husband was not there as he usually was to help her restrain herself. She was being regarded from two pairs of haughty eyes. "Coal merchant," she added.

"Yes." Lady Lovestone nodded. "Well, I hope you will be happy, I am sure, Lady Falloden. Indeed, I do not see how you could fail to be happy. Sir Hector might have been prevailed upon to allow Falloden to pay his addresses to Dorothea, you know, but he was shockingly low on funds. I daresay that situation has been remedied.''

''Yes,'' Eleanor said. ''Papa was dreadfully rich.'' She smiled at Dorothea Lovestone and wondered if the girl had loved her husband. And if he had loved her.

''Of course,'' Lady Lovestone said, ''there were other things, though I daresay they might have changed if he had married Dorothea. But such matters would not be of concern to you, I am sure, Lady Falloden. One advantage of not having a gentle upbringing, I always say, is that one does not have such tender sensibilities. It can be a dreadful thing to be too tender-hearted.''

''I daresay,'' Eleanor said, smiling. ''I would not know, ma'am, not having had a gentle upbringing.''

''And since you are in mourning for your poor dear papa anyway,'' Lady Lovestone said, ''I daresay you do not mind that Falloden goes out every evening without you. Dorothea has been brought up to expect evening entertainments. And of course he is very discreet, which must be a comfort. I have heard that his— ah—other interest is quite refined, though I know nothing about such creatures, of course.''

''Of course,'' Eleanor said, still smiling. ''Only enough to be able to share with the wives, ma'am. That is understandable. And you might hurt them if you knew too many details, after all. If the mistresses were prettier than they, for example, or more shapely. Or better performers in bed.''

''Dorothea, my love!'' Lady Lovestone said, her hand shooting to her heart while the girl squirmed with discomfort and stared saucer-eyed at Eleanor.

''It is not hurtful at all, but only enormously soothing,'' Eleanor said, ''to know that my husband's—ah— other interest is refined. She might be vulgar, after all, and that would be a dreadfully lowering thing.''

"Lady Falloden," Lady Lovestone said, "I pray you to remember that my daughter is present."

"I do beg your pardon." Eleanor smiled warmly at the girl and then at her mother. "But since you introduced the topic, ma'am, I assumed that you considered it a suitable one for your daughter's ears."

They talked of the weather for five minutes before Lady Lovestone rose to her feet and signaled to her daughter and they took their leave a full ten minutes before it would have been polite to do so.

They went away satisfied, Eleanor thought, sitting down straight-backed in the chair she had vacated in order to take leave of her visitors. All their suspicions had been confirmed. The Earl of Falloden had married the enormously vulgar daughter of a cit—for her money. They could boast forever that Dorothea would have been his choice if only Sir Hector could have been prevailed upon to overlook his penniless state and his monumental debts. They could now be happy. She had made their day complete.

She raised her half-empty cup of tea to her lips, but set it back in the saucer again untasted. Her hand was shaking. So he had a mistress, did he? She might have known it. He was, after all, a member of the decadent aristocracy. He could not be expected to have any of the stricter moral values of her own class. And he was certainly getting no sexual satisfaction from his wife.

She did not care. She really did not. Let him do those terrifying and painful things to someone who was paid well to endure them. Let him spend as many evenings as he wanted with his mistress. That would leave her free to be alone in her own domain. She did not care.

But her thoughts turned immediately to Aunt Beryl and Aunt Ruth and her cousins and her reasons for choosing them to invite to spend Christmas at Grenfell Park. She would be damned, she thought, anger rising to fury within her, before she would invite guests only on the grounds that they would be least likely to disturb her husband's sensibilities and those of his guests.

Oh, she would be damned before she would choose thusly.

She had asked him how many of her own guests she might invite, and he had replied that she might ask as many as she wanted. Well, then. He had had a chance to put a limit on the number, but he had unwisely neglected to do so.

Eleanor got to her feet, a rather grim smile on her lips. The escritoire and the writing paper and pens were in the morning room. She had a busy few hours ahead of her.

6

He was rather looking forward to Christmas, the Earl of Falloden realized with some surprise. He had never particularly enjoyed the season. Even when he was a boy, when his parents were still alive, nothing much had been made of Christmas. He had had no brothers and sisters and his parents had liked to stay at home rather than seek out parties or invite guests. And when there had been guests, they had always been exclusively adult and he had been confined to the nursery. With his grandparents things has been much the same.

In more recent years he had gone wherever he was invited, sometimes to parties in the country homes of his friends, sometimes merely to dinners and balls in town. But he had always been glad when it was over. For some reason he had always felt lonely at Christmas, as if there should be a great deal more to it than he had ever experienced.

But this year he was looking forward to it. He would be at Grenfell Park, and he would be able to look around him and know that it was all his, without conditions attached, and that he could dream of all he wanted to do for the house and the park and the farms with the knowledge that at last he could make his dreams reality. He had spent many childhood holidays at Grenfell with his grandparents and had lived with them after his fourteenth year, after the death of his parents within a year of each other. He loved Grenfell.

And he was not sorry that he had invited guests when in his cups the week before his wedding. Bertie was coming, as were Lord Charles Wright; Jason, Viscount Sotherby; and the Honorable Mr. Timothy Badcombe. He had never had guests for Christmas. Perhaps their presence would make the season more enjoyable.

And strangely enough—very strangely—he was not averse to the prospect of being in the country with his wife. There had been a cautious peace between them since the morning after her father's death. They had not quarreled or spoken bitingly or with sarcasm to each other, except on very rare occasions, when the offending words were almost always followed immediately by an apology.

There was no affection between them, no friendship, no closeness at all. And yet the hostility had gone or at least had been pushed into the background. He had hopes that they could live together with civility for what remained of the first year of their marriage. And perhaps for longer. For he made a disturbing discovery during the first month of his marriage, and that was that he could not ignore the new state of his life. He could no longer feel like an unmarried man. And it was not just her presence in his home. It was her presence in his conscience.

After her father's funeral he took to going to White's each evening. But instead of enjoying himself there, as he had always used to do, he found himself thinking about the unfairness of life. His wife, being a woman, had no choice but to stay home alone since he was not escorting her anywhere. Her evenings must be unutterably dreary, he thought.

Twice he went to Alice's and bedded her both times. The second time he took her a gift, a ruby-studded bracelet, which he knew she would like. He had never before been able to buy her expensive gifts on whim. But guilt lay heavy on his heart as she exclaimed over it and had him clasp it about her wrist. It had been bought with money he had acquired with his marriage. And his wife was sitting home alone.

"It is a parting gift," he told Alice abruptly. And realized as he waited for dismay to overtake him at speaking so impulsively that he did not feel dismay at all. Only relief.

He had not bought his wife any gifts at all. Eleanor. Somehow he found it difficult to think of her by name. He could not bring himself to call her by name.

They were going to go into the country together for Christmas. They were going to stay there for the better part of a year. Perhaps, he thought, he would make a real effort to get to know her, to discover if there was anything but coldness and waspishness behind the calm, unsmiling appearance she always presented to him. Perhaps he would even begin to live with her as his wife, though it would be difficult to go to her bed again when he had not done so since their wedding night.

If his promise to her father compelled him to spend a year with her anyway, he thought, then he might as well use that time getting his heir on her if he could. If he could get her with child within the year, and if the child turned out to be a boy, then there would be no further necessity for them to live together if he found after all that nothing could be made of their marriage.

He was going to give it a try anyway. And what better time was there to try to inject a little warmth into their relationship than Christmas? He only hoped that she had invited a friend or two. It might be a difficult situation otherwise—five men and one lady.

"We will leave for Grenfell Park next week," he told her one evening when they were sitting, as they had done for five evenings in a row, in the library after dinner. He might even have enjoyed those evenings, he sometimes thought, except that he could never think of any topic of conversation that might have drawn them into a cozy chat. They never chattered, only conversed very deliberately on impersonal topics. "I will need to inform the housekeeper how many guests will be expected for Christmas."

She raised her eyes from her book. And raised her chin a notch in a gesture he recognized from earlier days. Then it had usually been the herald to some sarcasm or some defiance.

"I hope you have invited a friend or two," he said.

"One or two?" she said. "You did not impose a limit on the number I might invite, my lord."

"You have invited more, then?" he said. "Good."

"You are not afraid," she asked, "that your friends will object to sharing your home with people from my world?"

She looked and sounded as if she were on the verge of quarreling with him again, he thought. Just like a hedgehog.

"If they do," he said, looking steadily back at her, "then they will have me to deal with. You are my wife."

"And any slight to me would be a slight to you," she said. "Of course. I am honored."

"That was uncalled for, my lady," he said.

"Yes." She looked down at her book again.

"Whom have you invited?" he asked. "How many?"

"My family," she said, glaring at him suddenly, daring him to object, the color high on her cheekbones. "We have always spent holidays together whenever possible. And this is a special holiday. It is the first Christmas without my father. And I promised him that I would make it a wonderful one. But doubtless you will think it inappropriate to have a family celebration less than two months after his death."

He wondered with the beginnings of unwilling anger how many other fictitious promises to her father she would invent over the coming weeks and months. Obviously she was a woman who craved a life of gaiety and was not going to allow respect for a dead father to get in her way. "We can celebrate in a subdued manner," he said.

"Not with my family," she said. "They are the loudest, most boisterous—most vulgar—crowd you could possibly imagine."

The anger built. "Exactly how many are we talking about?" he asked.

She was silent for a few moments, her eyes lowered. But he could tell by the slight movement of her fingers that she was counting, doing a mental review of the relatives she had invited.

"Twenty," she said, looking back up at him coolly, "counting Cousin Tom's two children. Is that too many, my lord? Should I have assumed when you said that I might invite any number that you meant no more than four?"

"Twenty," he repeated. *Good God.*

"It is a dreadful prospect, is it not," she said, "to think of Grenfell Park, seat of the Earl of Falloden, being overrun by businessmen and merchants and farmers? Rather like cattle being let loose in the nave of a cathedral. But you must remember, my lord, that Grenfell Park has been paid for and will continue to be paid for with a merchant's money."

He stayed in his chair. If he got to his feet, he thought, he might show his fury in deeds as well as in words.

"I am not likely to forget it this side of the grave, my lady," he said. "Not with a shrew of a wife to remind me constantly."

"Well," she said, "you can always escape from me, my lord. You can always take yourself beyond the range of my shrewish tongue. I am told she is refined. That must be a comfort to you."

"*Who* is refined?" he asked, his eyes narrowing.

"Your mistress," she said. "The woman with whom you take your pleasure."

"Ah," he said. "And who was kind enough to inform you that she is refined, pray?"

"The mother of the girl you loved—or love, perhaps—and were too impoverished to marry."

"Lady Lovestone," he said. "Yes, I loved Dorothea and would have married her too if circumstances had been different. She is beautiful and sweet and tender-hearted.'' He felt a pang of longing for the sweetness and refinement he might have had in a wife.

"All the things I am not," she said.

"The words are your own," he told her coldly.

"And doubtless you would have given up your mistress for her and lived happily ever after," she said. "How unfortunate that you are a spendthrift, my lord, and like to play deep at gaming and have not a great deal of good luck. And how fortunate for me. I might never have won myself such a noble husband if you had learned to live within your means."

"Fortunate you might call it," he said, getting to his feet at last. "You have my title and all that comes with it for the rest of your life. But you will never have one corner of my heart or my liking or my respect. Or my company, either, whenever I can help it." He bowed deeply to her. "Enjoy your triumph, my lady. I hope—I sincerely hope—it will prove to be an empty one."

"And I hope," she said through her teeth as he strode toward the door, "that my father's money brings you not one ounce of happiness, my lord. I sincerely hope it."

Something smashed violently as he closed the door of the library behind him. He guessed that in her passion she had hurled something, probably the porcelain figurine from the table beside her, across the room.

"My coat and hat," he said curtly to the footman in the hall.

"Shall I send for your carriage, my lord?" the man asked with a bow.

"I shall walk," he said, restraining the urge to bark at the man, who had done nothing to offend, and he strode out through the door one minute later, his greatcoat still unbuttoned despite the evening chill and the brisk wind. But he could not even go to Bertie to pour out his venom and his frustration, he realized. She was his wife and this was his marriage. A private business. Not one he could discuss with a friend. He thought of Dorothea again as he buttoned his coat and pulled on his gloves hastily. He could not remember ever having felt more lonely than he felt at that moment.

There were fewer than two weeks left before Christmas, she told herself, gazing out of the carriage window on unfamiliar countryside made drab by a heavy gray sky and a semi-dusk despite the fact that the afternoon was no more than half gone. There was no feeling of Christmas. Usually there was. Usually she took a maid and went shopping several times, not so much because she could not have purchased everything all at once, but because she liked the atmosphere of the shops and streets. She had always particularly liked Oxford Street at Christmas.

Perhaps it was because her father was recently dead, she thought. Undoubtedly that was the reason. And thinking about him, she felt the now-familiar aching in her chest and throat and the equally familiar sense of guilt. She had been unable to mourn for him. She had not once cried for him. She looked down at her blue velvet cloak, the one she had worn at her wedding. She had even put off her black mourning clothes when they left London. So had her husband, but she noticed that he wore a black armband. She did not. Tomorrow Papa would have been dead one month.

Or perhaps, she thought, it was because she was recently married and yet was already very unhappily married. They were seated side by side in the carriage, yet they had exchanged scarcely a word since leaving London, only the essential civilities. She was curious about the countryside, anxious and eager for her first glimpse of Grenfell Park, wondering how much farther there was to go. And yet she could not ask him. They had scarcely spoken in the five days since their quarrel.

She had wanted to apologize for that. Her behavior had been unpardonable. He had been quite justified in calling her a shrew. She had started it all, she had been forced to admit. Though he had looked stunned when she had told him there were twenty members of her family coming for Christmas—and indeed she had been surprised at the number when she had added it up—he had not made any objection either about the number or the character of his guests. Perhaps he would have had she given him time, but the point was that he had not before she decided to quarrel with him—her usual self-defense when she felt nervous or embarrassed.

She had wanted to apologize also for the smashed figurine, which had been one of her favorite pieces in the house. But she had not seen him again that evening or all the next day and the day after that only briefly. And he had bowed to her with distant formality and looked at her with cold, haughty eyes and spoken in a voice to match. And she had remembered the reason she had invited so many and the reason her nerves had been so brittle in the library that evening and the evenings before it.

He had a mistress. He did *that* with another woman when he had a wife. Not that she cared, of course. She would a thousand times rather he did it with someone else than with her. But even so, for five days she had felt unlovely and unattractive and lonely, although she had told herself her life was as she wished it to be. She did not want him anywhere near her bed, except that she wanted a child. And she spent five days wanting Wilfred and trying not to think about him. And five days remembering the blond and delicate Dorothea Lovestone.

So she had hardened her heart and not apologized. And it was too late now. Too late to restore even the less than satisfactory civility to their dealings together.

She was startled out of her black thoughts by the sight of a solitary horseman beside the road, his horse held stationary while he looked toward the approaching carriage. A highwayman, she thought, and was about to turn to her husband to give the alarm. But the rider turned his horse's head and galloped off ahead of them. He must have been merely uncertain of his direction, she thought.

How much farther?

"We will be at the village in a few minutes' time," her husband said suddenly, as if he had read her thoughts, "and at the house ten minutes after that."

It was the most he had said all at once since their journey began. Perhaps in the last week. She did not turn her eyes away from the window.

"We will be here for the next year," he said. "This is the place and these are the people with whom you will grow familiar, my lady. I believe it would be as well for us to forget about the past week, to put it behind us. Since we must endure each other's company, we might as well do it with a measure of civility."

She swallowed. He was holding out an olive branch again.

"And next week we will have guests to entertain," he said. "Twenty-four of them, to be exact. It would be churlish of us to be so at odds with each other that we cannot give them a happy Christmas. Do you not agree?"

"Yes," she said.

"Very well, then," he said. There was a short silence. "I put an end to my liaison with Alice Freeman a few days before you spoke to me about her. I beg your pardon for not having done so before our marriage."

She felt only humiliation. When she had spoken so shrewishly, he had already finished with his mistress. And he had begged her pardon. She wanted to beg his for having broken their agreement, for having given them both a week of silence and unpleasantness. She searched around in her head for suitable words.

But her attention was distracted. Bells? Even over the noise of the carriage and horses, she could hear bells pealing.

"Oh, Lord," her husband said, "I was afraid of this."

She looked at him inquiringly.

"If you have any smiles in you, my lady," he said,

"you had better don them now. We are about to be given a traditional country welcome."

"What?" She stared at him blankly.

"The Earl of Falloden is arriving home with his new bride," he said. "We must be greeted accordingly. I wonder how they knew we were approaching."

The horseman, Eleanor thought. And she felt her heart thumping as the carriage entered a village street and she saw that every window and door was hung with white bows and every inhabitant seemed to be out on the street, some of them waving handkerchiefs, all of them smiling broadly.

"Smile!" her husband commanded. "And raise your hand in greeting."

Eleanor obeyed. And for the first time had some realization of how her marriage was to change her life, of what it meant to be a countess.

The carriage drew to a halt outside the village inn and a clerical gentleman was bowing to her as her husband handed her out and a lady was curtsying at his side. The Reverend Jeremiah Blodell was honored to make the acquaintance of her ladyship, the Countess of Falloden, and he begged the honor of presenting his good wife, Mrs. Blodell. Eleanor checked her first impulse, which was to reach out her right hand, and inclined her head instead, smiling at the vicar and his wife.

And then her husband extended his arm and led her through the lobby of the inn, where two maids in mobcaps curtsied to the ground, up the stairs to the assembly rooms, and out onto the balcony that overlooked the street. It was not a large village, but it seemed to Eleanor that every inhabitant must be in the street below. To her it looked to be a dense enough crowd. Someone called for three cheers, and the crowd complied with enthusiasm.

When they quietened down, her husband took her by the hand and presented her to the crowd as his bride and the new Countess of Falloden. After the cheer that greeted his announcement and his brief words of thanks for the warm welcome home, the Reverend Blodell delivered a lengthy speech, which Eleanor was too agitated to listen to. It was succeeded by more cheering. She raised her hand in one brief wave, and someone in the crowd whistled.

The two maids in mobcaps and two menservants were carrying trays of champagne and cakes into the assembly rooms when they left the balcony and came back inside. And the village's leading citizens and some of the more prosperous tenant farmers were coming upstairs.

For the next ten minutes she clung to her husband's arm as he presented her to what seemed like a dizzying number of people and she tried desperately to store names and their matching faces in her memory. It was a skill her father had always impressed upon her. In business, he had said, it was a wise practice to remember the name even of someone one had met once ten years before. It made a good impression. It suggested to people that one cared for more than just deals and money.

Most of the people who had come to drink toasts to her health and her husband's and to eat cakes were the village businessmen—the butcher, the blacksmith, the haberdasher, and others. Eleanor gradually relaxed when she realized that there was nothing at all threatening about these people, that they were prepared to like and even admire her. Even if they knew her origins, she thought, they seemed not to care. Perhaps they liked the idea of having a countess who might be more accessible to them than the daughter of a peer might have been.

She slipped her hand from her husband's arm and engaged the butcher and a farmer and their wives in conversation. And then she was talking with the spinster daughter of a former vicar and the schoolteacher and Mrs. Blodell, and then with another group of people.

Suddenly she felt very happy. Almost deliriously so. She felt as if she was coming home even though she had never been to this place before or seen any of these people. And even though she had not yet seen Grenfell Park. And she was glad that they were to stay there for a year, that they would not be returning to London after Christmas. Even though London had always been her home and she had thought that she could not possibly be content anywhere else for very long, she no longer wanted to be in London. She had been unhappy there for the past month.

Perhaps, she thought with a hope born of the moment, things would be different now they were in the country. She glanced across the room at her husband, who was laughing at something the innkeeper was telling him. She could not remember seeing him laugh before. He looked boyish and carefree and very, very handsome. Something inside her turned over, painfully and unexpectedly.

They were on their way again eventually, leaving behind the village and turning almost immediately between massive stone gateposts and past twin gatehouses and proceeding along a winding elm drive through a heavier dusk.

"I should have warned you," her husband said from beside her. "But I had no idea the old custom would still be observed. The last bride to be brought here was my grandmother. I hope you were not dreadfully embarrassed. You did well."

Condescension again. Had he not expected her to do well? "They were my kind of people," she said. But she heard the sarcasm in her voice and regretted it. Perhaps she really would turn into a shrew if she were not careful, she thought. "I like them, my lord. They were very kind."

"Well," he said, "you had better not relax too much, my lady. If preparations were made for an elaborate welcome in the village, I am quite sure the same will hold true of the house. The servants will doubtless be lined up in the great hall and we will be expected to inspect them and to stop and speak with some of them. There will be more cheers and applause. Don't put your smile away just yet.''

She looked at him, but he had the side of his face almost against the glass and was gazing ahead—probably for the first sight of the house. All the servants of a grand house to greet? There was a fluttering of nervousness in her stomach. And a certain welling of excitement too.

For one moment she felt a deep regret that theirs was not a normal marriage, that he could not share with her his excitement at seeing his home again, that she could not share with him her excitement at discovering that this new home of hers felt like home even before she had seen it. It would have been lovely to be able to hold hands and smile at each other.

But at least, she thought, his words earlier had restored the civility to their relationship. She must be thankful for small mercies.

And he no longer had a mistress. And had apologized for having one at all after his marriage to her.

7

All their guests were to arrive four days before Christmas. The earl's own friends were to have come a week before, but he had put them off. He had even given them the chance to withdraw altogether, being careful to explain that Christmas at Grenfell was to be a large family gathering—his wife's family. And yet, incredibly, all four of them were still planning to come.

"After all, Falloden," Lord Charles Wright had said, more honest than the other three, "none of us has anywhere else to go, and Christmas is the most dreary time of year to be alone."

He was right. It was the worst time of all. Lord Charles had no family to speak of, certainly none that would welcome him for the holiday. Bertie had a mother and sisters, but their lives centered around their children, he always said. He always felt out of place and wary of their matchmaking energies turning on him. Badcombe had quarreled with his father and brother years before and had been told never to come home again. Sotherby had been married for two years when his wife died in childbed. His family lived close to the Scottish border.

Only Bertie had seemed a little wary of coming. "Perhaps your wife won't like it, Randolph," he had said. "Newly married and all that."

"But she knows of my four guests," the earl had said, "and has invited twenty of her own."

Sir Albert had looked taken aback. "I don't know," he had said. "Perhaps I had better lay my head on the chopping block before Mama and the girls this year after all.''

"Bertie," the earl had said, "don't desert me in my hour of need. Four against twenty. Think of it. And you are supposed to be my best friend." It was the closest he had come to breaking the confidentiality of his marriage and admitting that all was not well. "She obviously was not Pamela Hutchins' vulgar friend after all, by the way, was she?''

"No," his friend had said vaguely. "These twenty people are your wife's family, Randolph? I didn't know she had brothers and sisters.''

"Aunts and uncles and cousins, I gather," the earl had said. "Apparently they are a close family, Bertie. They spend holidays together and all that. I am looking forward to meeting them all," he had added gallantly and not quite truthfully. "All twenty of them, including two children.''

"Lord.'' Sir Albert had winced and scratched his head. "They will probably all be asking favors of you, Randolph. It must seem a grand thing to them that one of their number has crashed into our ranks. There are probably all sorts of eligible and hopeful female cousins among their number.''

The earl had stiffened. "It must be remembered," he had said, "that my wife's father gave me Grenfell, Bertie, and a great deal besides.''

"Ho.'' His friend had eyed him with interest. "Prickly, are you, Randolph? Touchy on the subject? Sorry, old chap.''

"She is my wife," the earl had said. "My countess, Bertie.''

Sir Albert had exhaled loudly. "It is important to you that I come, then, Randolph?" he had asked. "And I did promise, did I not? Oh, well, it will be an experience, I suppose.''

It was not exactly an enthusiastic acceptance, but the earl felt the need of those four friends of his, especially Bertie, his closest friend. And it should indeed be an experience, he thought in the days leading up to the arrival of their guests. Loud and boisterous, she had called them. And vulgar. Sometimes he felt almost panic-stricken.

But there was not much time to brood. While there was still time before the arrival of the guests and the close approach of Christmas, he spent time with his steward, going over the books with him and traveling about his farms. It was work that he suddenly enjoyed because it was all his now with no fear of loss, and he could listen to the complaints and suggestions of his steward and tenants with an open mind. He could agree to make improvements where they were needed, knowing that he had the money to cover the costs. He could even make a few suggestions of his own. And when he reviewed the rents paid by some of his poorer tenants, he could agree to lower them.

There were calls to be made and some to receive, sometimes alone and sometimes with his wife. They did not see a great deal of each other—not because they deliberately avoided each other, he felt, but because she was as busy as he. The schoolteacher wanted her to visit the school and listen to the children read. Their neighbors wanted to entertain her and to visit her. The vicar's wife wanted her to help with the children's Christmas concert.

And she wanted to spend time with the housekeeper, learning the workings of the house, learning to take charge of its running herself. She wanted to find out who the elderly and the sick were so that she might visit them regularly and take them Christmas hampers. She wanted to take Christmas hampers to all his farm laborers and their families.

He was impressed. She was behaving almost as if she had been brought up to know the life and duties of a lady. And he was intrigued to find her well received in the neighborhood and in the house. The servants all appeared to adore her after she had spent longer than an hour on their arrival speaking with each one of them, even Sally the scullery maid, who limped and had a speech impediment. She had talked softly to Sally and smiled a great deal. He had not known until the day of their arrival that she could smile. And that she looked incredibly lovely when she did so.

He was glad, he thought after a few days, that they had come into the country. It seemed to suit them both. He had been afraid that, creature of the city as she was, she would be unable to settle at Grenfell. But the outdoor walks and drives she took every day soon brought a glow to her cheeks, and he was reminded of how confined to home she had been after the death of her father.

Of course, the thought reminded him that she was showing precious little grief for her father. But that thought aside, he began to have cautious hopes that they would be able to live together for a year almost amicably. If only the arrival of her family and his friends did not upset matters. He dreaded their arrival, if the truth were known.

He almost decided to go to her on the night of their arrival. It would be an appropriate time, he thought, to turn over a new leaf and resume their marriage in its full sense. It would not seem odd, perhaps, to go to her now when everything was strange and different from the way it had been since their wedding. And he did not find the idea of bedding her repugnant. Rather the contrary. He wanted her, he realized with some surprise. He desired his wife. He remembered the passion of their wedding night with quickened breath.

But as he stood with his hand on the knob of the door that connected their dressing rooms and lifted the other hand to knock, he heard her talking with her maid at the other side of the door and even laughing. She sounded happy. It was a strange sound. He could not quite picture his wife laughing and happy. Perhaps, he thought suddenly, she had been like that all the time before he married her. Perhaps it was he who had taken away her warmth and her laughter—or else her ambition to ally herself with an available peer of the realm.

He would wait, he thought at first, until her maid had left. He set his forehead against the door and closed his eyes, trying to imagine how she would receive him. With gladness? Hardly that. With indifference? He would be chilled by indifference. With hostility? Would he see her chin come up and the martial gleam leap to her eyes? And would he then know that she awaited any opportunity there might be to say something scathing, to quarrel with him until he retaliated with cold insults? And would the result of it all be a repetition of what had happened on their wedding night—a fight for mastery on his part and for he knew not what on hers?

It would be a dreadful beginning to their new life in the country. A dreadful herald to Christmas. Perhaps they would not be able to recover from another quarrel in time to be hospitable to their guests. And that was going to be difficult enough, heaven knew. He would leave it, he decided at last. Perhaps after Christmas. Perhaps when all their guests had left and they were quiet and alone together again, it would seem almost natural to make of their marriage a more real thing. He turned reluctantly back to his bedchamber and lay awake and restless for a long time before falling asleep.

But on the whole, he thought before their guests arrived, things were going quite reasonably well. His marriage was not quite the nightmare it had started out to be.

The guests arrived before the snow. And the imminence of snow took them by surprise.

"Look," her husband said that morning at breakfast, gazing toward the windows, "those are snow clouds, I am sure. We are going to have snow for Christmas."

"Oh," she said, her gaze following his, "do you think so? But it never snows for Christmas. Early in December, maybe, and certainly in January. But never for Christmas."

"This year will be the exception," he said. "I would wager on it. But I hope everyone gets here first."

"It will be brown slush by tomorrow anyway," she said.

He looked at her and smiled. "This is the country, my lady," he said, "not London. Here the snow remains white as it is meant to be. And it hangs on the trees and blows into snowbanks to the delight of children of all ages and can be traversed only by sleigh—with jingling bells, of course."

"Oh, how wonderful!" she said wistfully. "Are you sure they are not rain clouds, my lord? Are you ever wrong?"

"I am infallible," he said. "Next only to God."

It was the only time he had said anything remotely playful to her. She smiled at him a little uncertainly.

But the guests arrived during the afternoon, and the snow did not begin to sift down until the evening and did not empty its load in earnest until the night.

Sir Albert Hagley arrived first with Viscount Sotherby. The viscount took her hand in his after her husband had introduced them and smiled at her and raised her hand to his lips.

"How kind of you to be willing to have us here with your family, Lady Falloden," he said. "My own family is very far away, I'm afraid."

She liked him immediately and breathed a silent sigh of relief. At least one of her husband's aristocratic friends was not going to look along the length of his nose at her. Sir Albert Hagley did not quite do that, of course, but she thought that they were probably both conscious of the time at that disastrous summer party when he had tried to flirt with her, even going so far as to allow his arm to brush against her breast when they were out walking, and she had told a slightly improper story one of her father's associates had once been scolded for telling in her presence. She had told it with a loud and broad cockney accent and laughed uproariously afterward. He had kept his distance for the rest of their time there, but she had not dropped either the cockney accent or the loudness. He was not the only gentleman who had tried to take liberties with her.

He greeted her now as he had greeted her on her wedding day, with eyes that did not quite meet hers, and with exaggerated courtesy. And he turned in some relief to greet her husband more heartily. She wished that he had found some excuse not to come. But he was her husband's friend—and she was not going to allow his presence to dampen her spirits. Certainly not. She lifted her chin.

Uncle Sam Transome, Papa's eldest brother, arrived next with Aunt Irene and Cousin Tom and his wife, Bessie, and their two children, Davie and Jenny. Uncle Sam grew larger and rounder and more florid of complexion every time she saw him, Eleanor thought, exclaiming in delight when they all came up the house steps and into the great hall and he spread his arms to hug her and squeezed until she thought every last ounce of air must be gone from her lungs.

"Ellie!" he boomed. "As pretty as a picture and as elegant as any lady. And a lady indeed. Am I to call you 'my lady' now and curtsy to you, heh? Eh, Irene? What's that? Speak up. Oh, "bow," is it? I am to bow to you, Ellie? I am sorry about your papa, girl. More sorry than I can say. A fine man was Joe, and the most successful of the lot of us. And generous, Ellie. Always generous. I miss him sorely." He hugged her tightly again.

They were not wearing mourning, Eleanor noticed in relief as she relaxed into his embrace and breathed in the familiar scents of leather and pipe tobacco. They had acceded to her express wish and Papa's.

She extricated herself finally and raised a flaming face to her silent and impassive husband. What must he be thinking? She made the introductions. "Uncle Samuel is a butcher, my lord," she added with a small lift of the chin. "He has probably the most successful butcher's business in Bristol."

"That I do, lad, that I do," Uncle Sam said modestly, taking her husband's hand in his large paw and wringing it. "And 'my lord,' is it?" He winked ostentatiously. "I'll wager it's not always that when you are private together, eh, lad?"

Eleanor felt the inappropriate urge to giggle and wondered when her husband had last been addressed as a lad. He talked courteously with Aunt Irene and Tom and Bessie and exchanged a word with each of the children before turning them over to Mrs. Turner, a temporary nurse recruited from the village.

And then everyone else seemed to arrive together, so that the afternoon was swallowed up with greetings and smiles and shaking hands and treks upstairs with the housekeeper and down again eventually for tea in the lower salon.

The Honorable Mr. Timothy Badcombe was a thin and serious young man, who nevertheless did not seem too disconcerted to find himself in the great hall at the same time as Uncle Ben Transome and Aunt Eunice and Cousin Rachel. Uncle Ben was almost as large and almost as loud as Uncle Sam, though his claim was always that he could never get in a word edgewise when Aunt Eunice was around. Uncle Ben was the innkeeper of a prosperous posting inn outside Bristol.

He too hugged Eleanor as if to break every bone in her body and murmured sympathy in her ear for the loss of her father. Aunt Eunice kissed her and Rachel took her hand and squeezed it.

"Papa cried dreadfully, Ellie," she whispered. "And so did Mama and I. Uncle Joe was my very favorite uncle even though I love Uncle Sam dearly too. Poor Ellie. But what a splendid marriage."

Eleanor squeezed her hand in return. There was no chance for a lengthier exchange with her favorite cousin.

Lord Charles Wright arrived at almost the same moment as Aunt Beryl Weekes and Aunt Ruth Transome, sisters of Eleanor's father, and Cousins Muriel and Mabel Weekes. Aunt Ruth, who had obviously got herself into a taking at the grandeur of being an invited guest at the home of an earl, mistook Lord Charles for her host, and a great number of voices, each pitched slightly louder than the one before, were necessary before she discovered who was the true Earl of Falloden and husband of her dear Ellie. Then she proceeded to weep in Eleanor's arms for the best brother in all the world.

"And, I will be bound, the dearest papa too, dear," she said.

Aunt Beryl explained in strident tones that Aunt Ruth had had palpitations that very morning at the thought of coming to Grenfell Park, though why she should have taken on so when they had been accustomed to dining with Lord Sharples while the late Mr. Weekes had been one of his more prominent tenant farmers Aunt Beryl could not explain.

Eleanor glanced several times at her husband, her chin lifted, expecting his contempt. But there was nothing except careful courtesy in his expression.

And then, just a little later, Aunt Catherine Gullis, sister of Eleanor's mother, arrived with Uncle Harry and Cousins George, Susan, Harvey, and Jane. Uncle Harry was a very successful cloth merchant in Bristol and almost as wealthy as Papa had been. His grandfather was a baronet and he had taken with the greatest good humor a good deal of ribbing for the fact from Papa and Uncle Sam and Uncle Ben. Aunt Catherine held Eleanor wordlessly in her arms.

"Poor Ellie," she said at last. "A brilliant marriage and the passing of your poor papa all at once, dear. It must be very bewildering."

And then on their heels came Cousin Aubrey Ellis, a tenant farmer—actually Papa's cousin, who had grown up almost as a brother to him. Uncle Aubrey was a widower. But he had not come alone. And after all there were to be twenty-one members of her family as guests. Cousin Aubrey's son had come uninvited.

Wilfred. Looking tall and slim and very blond. With fire burning in his eyes as he took her hand in his and leaned forward to kiss her on the cheek.

"I thought you would not mind my coming, Ellie,"

he said rather loudly, "since the family is always together on such occasions. Indeed, Papa and I agreed that your invitation was probably intended to include me."

"Of course it was," the earl said, holding out his right hand. "We fully intended that every member of my wife's family be here to celebrate Christmas with us." He looked inquiringly at her.

"Wilfred Ellis, my lord," she said. "My second cousin. A shipping clerk in Bristol."

"Oh, no longer anything so lowly, Ellie," he said, setting his hand in her husband's. "I have been given a partnership. Did you not know?"

"No," she said. "I did not know. Congratulations, Wilfred."

Too late. Not quite two months too late. Had this happened two months before, he would have answered her letter differently. He would have had the position and the income as a partner in the company to make her his bride. She felt as if she were suffocating. She thought of the kisses they had shared and the love promises they had exchanged during the summer at Muriel Weekes' coming-of-age party. She willed her mind to blankness and looked at her husband, who was turning over the last of the arrivals to the housekeeper's care with all the graciousness of his rank.

And then suddenly they were alone together in the hall, though sounds of animated conversation were coming from the salon. She looked into his eyes and raised her chin.

"Everyone has arrived safely before the snow, and for that we must be thankful," he said.

He looked so elegant and quiet and refined, she thought, the hall seeming very silent after the boisterous and almost chaotic arrivals of all her family members. She felt very much on the defensive. It was not that she was ashamed of her family, she assured herself. She certainly was not. She loved them all dearly as she always had. But they were from a totally different world from that inhabited by her husband. And she did not wish to see them through his eyes. She wished now that she had not invited them.

"I am not ashamed of them," she almost hissed at him. "Don't expect me to be."

His eyebrows lifted and his eyes turned cold and they looked back intently into hers. "Was there any need of that?" he asked. "Have I been playing the part of haughty aristocrat, my lady? Have I shown any signs of condescension—or contempt?"

"No," she said. "Of course not. You are a gentleman." And as such an expert in hiding his feelings.

"Ah," he said. "It is that fact alone that has helped me mask my scorn, is it?"

She said nothing. She wished fervently that she had not started this. What did his opinion matter anyway?

"Well," he said, "at least you will have that consolation in the coming days, my lady. At least you will know that I am too genteel to reveal my disgust at having to share my home with a crowd of vulgar tradesmen and such. An innkeeper? Goodness me. And a butcher? The mind shudders. But only the mind. The body and the voice will remain courteous."

She had started it. She could hardly blame him. But she could not apologize, either. What if he spoke the truth? What if he really did despise her family—the people who had always made up her world? Well, what if he did? She was making her own misery, she knew, but could not seem to do anything about it.

He was holding out an arm for hers and bowing to her. "Shall we join our guests?" he asked.

She set her arm on his and they entered the salon together. And smiled—about them but not at each other.

Wilfred had come, she thought with a great sinking of the heart. He was upstairs at that very moment. Soon he would come down and she would be forced to look at him and converse with him and smile at him. Just as if he had never been any more than a cousin to her. Just as if the mind would not be making comparisons.

For the first time since her arrival at Grenfell Park, happiness had deserted her utterly, leaving leaden depression in its place. She suddenly missed her father. The missing him was like a fist slamming against her stomach, robbing her of breath.

Playing the part of courteous and sociable host did not always come easy, the Earl of Falloden found during tea and later during dinner. He had somehow expected that his wife's family would be awed at the fact that they were guests at Grenfell Park, their host an earl. He had expected to have to use all his social skills to set them at their ease. Even the boisterous arrivals during the afternoon and the cheerful conversation during tea had not quite alerted him to the truth. As soon as they were all seated at the dinner table in a more formal setting, he had believed, they would all freeze.

It was with some amazement, then, that he discovered that conversation at the table was lively and noisy, with a great deal of laughter and several raised voices. Not many of his guests observed the genteel rule that one converse only with one's immediate neighbors. Uncle Sam and Uncle Ben in particular, who were seated at opposite sides and almost opposite ends of the table, often felt it necessary to exchange witticisms. And each one aroused a general burst of laughter.

His friends were looking amused, the earl found when he glanced at them curiously. Except Bertie, who was deep in conversation with Rachel Transome. Uncle Ben's daughter? Yes, Uncle Sam had only the married son—Tom. The earl was diligently trying to sort out his in-laws. His in-laws. These people were all related to him by marriage, he told himself incredulously. The fact had still not quite sunk home.

He glanced at his wife, who sat opposite him at the foot of the long table. She too was smiling until she caught his eye and the smile faded and she looked at him defiantly.

Had she done it all deliberately? he wondered. Had she invited her whole family to join them during their first Christmas at Grenfell Park in the hope of discomfiting him? Or had she invited them merely because they were her family and she needed them with her this first Christmas without her father? But the answer was obvious. She showed no sign of grieving, but the lift of her chin showed clearly that she was defying him.

He could have cheerfully shaken her. He had nothing against her relatives. Indeed, they were a remarkably cheerful lot. But even so he had no idea how he was to entertain them, since already it seemed clear that they were not going to conform themselves to any recognizable rules of behavior.

And he had been looking forward to Christmas for perhaps the first time in his life!

In the drawing room after dinner the entertainment looked after itself. He had been prepared to organize tables of cards for the older people and perhaps to encourage the younger people to gather about the pianoforte.

But Uncle Sam loudly demanded to know of his niece when Christmas was to begin, and in a moment everyone was making animated plans to raid his park the next day and drag inside all the greenery they could lay their hands on.

"Mistletoe?" his wife said in answer to one question. "Is there any in the neighborhood, my lord?"

There had always been a kissing bough in his grandparents' day. "There are oaks in the woods to the north of the house," he said. "I believe that is where the mistletoe used to come from."

It was settled, then. They would raid the woods as well as the park. And while they were about it, they would find a Yule log and drag it back to the house.

"After all," Uncle Ben said, "we cannot have Christmas without a Yule log, now can we, Randy?"

It took a moment for the earl to realize that he was the one being addressed. He pursed his lips and resisted the unexpected impulse to roar with laughter. *Randy?* He exchanged a glance with Bertie, or tried to do so, but Bertie was again in conversation with Rachel.

"Is that what we are to call you, dear?" Aunt Eunice asked, lifting her head from a group of ladies close to the fire. "I wondered. Now, where are the decorations, Randy? Those of us who would prefer to stay indoors tomorrow morning will sort through them and have them ready when everything is brought inside."

Good heavens. Decorations. Bows and bells and such? Were there any? But there had been some when he was a boy.

"In the attic, I daresay, ma'am," he said. "I shall have them brought down tomorrow."

"No need," she said. "We will go up ourselves and save the servants the trouble, won't we, Beryl and Irene? And do call me Aunt Eunice. And Catherine? You too, Ruth? Or will the dust set you to wheezing? I suppose there will be dust. There always is in attics."

The earl had planned to go shooting the next day with his four friends and any of his wife's relatives who cared to join them. But Sotherby, he could hear, was agreeing to accompany Tom and Bessie and their children to look for holly, and Wright and Badcombe were agreeing with Uncle Sam that yes, indeed, they would be delighted to help with the Yule log. They looked delighted too. The world, at least the world he knew, seemed to have gone mad, the earl thought. Good heavens—Transomes invading his home and his park while he stood by speechless.

He had the feeling that his home might not be his own again until after Christmas. And he looked about him with the feeling that perhaps he had stepped into a dream. The Transomes and the Weekeses and the Gullises had the strange skill, he noticed, of all being able to speak at once and yet listen at the same time.

George Gullis, he saw, had an eye for Mabel Weekes,
who was far from indifferent to him. Interesting.

Then, just when he thought he might have to step in
to organize the rest of the evening, the young people
wandered over to the pianoforte without having to be
encouraged to do so, and Susan Gullis sat down to
play. And before any time at all had passed, the room
was filled with music, or what might pass for music
to an uncritical listener, as the whole family sang
Christmas carols with gusty enthusiasm. Sotherby and
Badcombe were singing too, the earl saw. And for lack
of anything else to do, and because he felt conspicuous
with his mouth closed, he joined in.

This was certainly going to be the strangest Christmas he had ever experienced, the earl thought, his eyes
moving about the room until they came to rest on his
wife, who was standing beside the pianoforte with
Muriel and Mabel Weekes and the youngest Gullis
girl—Jane?—and the uninvited Wilfred. She was singing. It was all most strange. He remembered the quiet,
genteel Christmases of his grandparents' time.

This was his wife's family, he thought. This was the
life she knew. Gatherings like this were customary with
these people. Warm, happy, noisy gatherings. And she
was amongst them, part of them, one with them. For
the first time he had some insight into how strange her
new life must be for her. As strange as this life was
to him. There was something about it, though, he
thought. Something almost enticing. And she was part
of it.

There was a great deal he did not know about her,
he mused. A great deal. And he found, examining the
idea in his mind, that he wanted to know her. She was
his wife. He had lived with her for longer than a
month. He had even shared the intimacy of the marriage bed with her on one occasion. Yet she was in
effect a stranger to him.

But a lovely stranger. And a proud and prickly and
quarrelsome one. A challenge, no less. Gazing across
the room, he felt a stirring in his loins for her and a

stirring too in his heart. They had quarreled earlier that day and probably would quarrel again tomorrow. But he knew that for a while at least he would keep coming back for more. Despite everything. Despite her family.

The realization somehow warmed him, and he smiled down at Aunt Ruth and set her in a flutter by seating himself on the arm of her chair.

8

He had been right, she thought, sitting on the edge of her bed shivering at the first impact of air beyond the warm cocoon of her blankets and noticing the strange light coming through the curtains at her windows. Oh, he had been right. She forgot all about the chill of the room, which the newly built fire had not yet dispersed, and raced across to kneel on the window seat and push the curtains aside.

Her eyes widened. She had known—they had all known—that it was snowing last evening, but she had expected that as usually happened the snow would have turned to rain at some time during the night. She had expected nothing but a slushy landscape to ruin their hunt for Christmas greenery.

But what she saw made her want to jump with girlish glee. Snow everywhere, a thick blanket masking the outlines of everything, completely obliterating paths and driveway. Snow loading down the branches of the trees and piled inches thick on the sill outside her window. Snow sparkling in the weak sunlight as if by some magic it had been sprinkled with jewels.

"Oh," she said to the empty room. "Oh." And she scrambled off the window seat again and actually took a few steps toward her dressing room before realizing where she was going. She had been going to rush through into his rooms to share the wonder of it with him.

The very thought was enough to bring color flooding to her cheek. What on earth had possessed her? She had quarreled with him the day before because she had been afraid that he was ashamed of her family, and he had looked at her scathingly as he recalled Uncle Sam's and Uncle Ben's occupations. But she had started it. She was so afraid that he would feel nothing but contempt for them all.

But why should she fear such a thing? she asked herself for surely the dozenth time. Why did it matter to her? The very reason she had invited them all was to defy him because he had a mistress who was refined.

She looked down at her hands and felt depression threaten her mood again as she realized that she did care what he thought. He was her husband, after all, and despite herself she had felt proud the evening before to look about the drawing room and know that he was hers. Despite the fact that Wilfred had remained as close to her as he could. She had tried not to notice him. She tried now not to think of him.

But there was snow out there, she reminded herself, looking again at the window with bright eyes. And there were cousins to share it with. She rang the bell for her maid and hurried through to her dressing room.

And yet, she discovered a short while later when she came back into her room, wearing a warm wool dress, despite her haste she was not the first downstairs. She heard a shriek and sure enough, when she raced to the window, she saw that there were four people outside already. Oh, she was missing the fun, she thought as she ran back into her dressing room to find and to pull on a warm hooded cloak and gloves. And she tore down the stairs a few moments later and went out through the front doors, which a grinning footman held open for her. She did not even think to consider his expression impertinent. She grinned back as she passed.

Davie and Jenny were out there, taking runs and hurling themselves full length and facedown into the deep bank of soft snow that had drifted against the base of the fountain. Tom and Lord Charles were throwing snowballs at Muriel and Susan—two more persons had arrived since she looked out of the window.

But pausing at the top of the steps brought good sense back to Eleanor. Gracious, she was the Countess of Falloden and had been about to romp in the snow with her cousins for all the world to see—in particular her servants. It was true that she was a little less than twenty years old and true that she was younger than any of the four adults now engaged in a noisy snowball fight. But she was a married lady and married to an earl, no less.

A snowball landed with a thud against her shoulder and Lord Charles, of all people, stood grinning up at her. At the same moment more people came out through the doors behind her.

"I think we had better help the girls, Harve," George said. "They look to be in dire straits. Why are you standing here idle, Ellie?"

"I think I'll join the men," Rachel said. "Tom has deadly aim. I would rather have him on my side. Are you coming, Ellie?"

And before Eleanor knew quite what was happening or could give further consideration to her dignity, she felt both her arms being taken, one by George and the other, she saw when she looked, by a grinning Viscount Sotherby, and she was hurried down into the fray.

"Don't worry, Lady Falloden," the viscount said. "I'll fight on your side."

She lost track of time. It might have been ten minutes that passed or half an hour while snowballs whizzed through the air and men shouted and girls shrieked and everyone panted and laughed and giggled or hurled insults as well as snowballs at mortal enemies. More people came out. Uncle Sam appeared fighting on the other side, and Wilfred on hers. She smiled at him quickly before resuming the battle and yelled at Uncle Sam that it was against the rules to throw more than one snowball at a time.

"Eh?" he bellowed back, cupping one ear. "I'm

strangely deaf this morning, Ellie. Must be the snow. Here—catch!'' And a soft, wet lump of snow collided with her bosom.

And then the silent figure striding toward the house from the direction of the stables and coming to a halt at the bottom of the steps, his greatcoat and hat immaculate and quite free of snow. And the embarrassment and guilt and the restored knowledge that she had no business doing what she was doing. And the usual stubborn defiance and conviction that she did not care what he thought or what sort of chilly lecture he cared to give her later. She threw back her head and shrieked and stooped down to mold a fresh snowball.

It caught him somewhere on the jaw, halfway between his chin and his ear. It was the most horrid place of all for a snowball to land, for it would be impossible to brush it all away without at least some of it finding its way in an icy trickle down the neck. She looked at him and laughed and bent down for more snow, her eyes picking out Uncle Sam, who had scored a hit on her elbow a few moments before.

Then suddenly her feet disappeared from under her and she was shrieking and kicking them on air. It was Wilfred, she thought indignantly until she looked up to see who had scooped her into his arms and was striding with her away from the fight. He looked grim. Oh dear, she thought, now she was for it. She had wounded his aristocratic pride. She giggled.

But it was not quite in the direction of the house that he strode. Suddenly and quite alarmingly he swung her to one side and then tossed her so that she shrieked in good earnest and her arms and legs flailed uselessly as she flew through the air. She came to land deep in the snowbank that had been the children's playground earlier. And of course she landed with her mouth open and was soon sputtering and threshing about in a vain attempt to find her feet in the snow. It was too deep and too soft.

''Allow me, my lady.'' His voice was chilly, but the hand that was stretched out to her looked reassuringly solid, and the gleam in his eyes might have been anything from anger to triumph to amusement. She reached up a cautious hand and set it in his.

She came to her feet in such a hurried scramble that she stopped only when she came against the solid wall of his chest. She looked up into his face.

"Sometimes," he said, "it is more effective to take one's adversary to the snowball than the other way around. Especially when that adversary is unwise enough to laugh after scoring a direct hit."

She bit her lip, not sure whether to laugh or look contrite, and his eyes flickered down to follow the gesture. And heavens, she thought, she was still against his chest. Just as if she were incapable of standing on her own two feet. Which perhaps she was.

Then sounds of laughter penetrated her consciousness and she realized that this time everyone was laughing in unison. The fight had stopped and everyone had witnessed her toss in the snow. Most of the fighters were brushing at themselves and shaking coats and cloaks and slapping mittens together.

"That's the way, lad," Uncle Sam called out. "Treat 'em rough. They like it that way."

"Oh, Uncle Sam!" There was a chorus of indignant protests from the female cousins. Everyone knew that Uncle Sam always treated Aunt Irene as if she were a goddess from one of those old Greek stories, as Papa had always put it.

Eleanor pushed away from her husband, thoroughly uncomfortable, and brushed at her cloak, which was caked with snow. Heavens, for one moment she had thought that he was going to kiss her. She had felt a flaring of heat despite the fact that she had snow inside her clothing as well as outside. And then a large, firm hand was brushing at the back of her cloak and she felt the heat again.

"I think, my lady," he said, "we had better take our guests inside for breakfast if we are to gather Christmas greenery this morning."

"Yes," she said, taking his offered arm. The children, she saw, were building a snowman. Everyone else seemed to be talking all at once—a characteristic of her family.

Since there was to be no shooting after all and it was likely to be close to noon before everyone was up and ready to go out looking for Christmas greenery, the Earl of Falloden had decided to go out early and conduct some business that he would otherwise have had to fit in later in the day. He came home expecting to find only the most hardy of his guests beginning to drift down to the breakfast room.

Instead he discovered a sight the like of which he had never seen at Grenfell Park before and had never dreamed of seeing. All of his guests, almost without exception, were out on the terrace engaged in a vigorous and noisy snowball fight. Even three of his own friends were among them, he saw as he drew closer. And his wife.

His first reaction was one of discomfort. His grandmother would turn over in her grave! Everything had always been conducted with dignified propriety at Grenfell Park. And what would the servants think? Especially when they saw his wife out there with everyone else, shrieking and laughing and hurling with as much abandon as anyone else. But then, as he drew closer still and came to a halt at the foot of the steps leading up to the house, he felt a certain envy. Except for his years at school, he had been brought up very much alone. At home, both with his parents and with his grandparents, he had been expected to behave with quiet decorum. Even at Christmastime. Even when there was a fresh blanket of snow on the ground. He had never been encouraged to behave with spontaneity.

He felt envious and half inclined to join in the fun. And to hell with any servant who did not like to see their earl and countess frolicking in the snow, he thought recklessly a moment before a snowball shattered against his jaw and found an icy path down his

neck. He knew it had come from his wife's hand even
as she laughed and stooped to gather more snow.

He acted from pure instinct—something he almost
never did even now, more than nine years after the
death of his grandfather. He was not even quite sure
what he intended to do with her when he swept her up
into his arms and strode away from the battlefield with
her. But the snowbank was not to be resisted, he saw
almost immediately. He could not remember enjoying
a moment more than the one in which he tossed her
into it and watched her sail through the air, arms and
legs flapping in ungainly fashion, and land deep in the
soft snow.

He could have laughed aloud and would have done
so if she had not looked up at him with such wary
indignation. If she could have seen herself in a looking
glass at that moment, he thought, she would have
shuddered with mortification. Her cheeks and nose
were a shiny red, her hair was wet and marvelously
untidy beneath her hood, and she was totally covered
with snow. Even her eyebrows and eyelashes were
white.

And yet, he found when he had jerked her to her
feet and against his chest, he wanted her as he had
wanted her almost every moment since their arrival in
the country. Despite her less than immaculate appearance, she was beautiful. And something else had been
revealed to him. The countryside and the arrival of her
family had combined to reveal a warmth and a vi-
brance and a spontaneity in her that had him aching
with a longing for something he had never known. If
this was what she was really like, he thought, and not
the cold marble statue he had known in London . . .
The thought somehow interfered with his breathing.

Aunt Beryl, Aunt Eunice, and Aunt Ruth stayed at
the house to hunt out the decorations from the attic.
Everyone else came downstairs dressed for the outdoors.

"Wrap that scarf warmly about your neck," Aunt

Beryl told the earl with maternal solicitude. "You do not want to have a chill over Christmas."

The earl agreed meekly that he did not and wrapped obediently.

"Don't worry about a thing here, Randy," Aunt Eunice told him. "We will have everything organized by the time you get back."

He had no doubt that they would.

"Ellie, dear," Aunt Ruth whispered, hugging her niece, "such a very handsome gentleman. Dear Joseph did well for you. And not at all high and mighty, which I rather feared, him being an earl and all that. Did you see him sit on the arm of my chair last evening just as if he were one of the family? Which of course he is, though it was very obliging of him all the same. Oh, bless my soul, and just think of it. Little Ellie a countess."

Little Ellie, who was a few inches taller than her aunt, bent to kiss her cheek.

"You must be very happy, dear," Aunt Ruth said with a sigh.

"I am, Aunt," Eleanor said with a smile, and for the moment she did not lie. Her husband was laughing at something Uncle Harry had said, and he did look almost like one of the family. Almost.

Jenny rode on her father's shoulders while Davie waded along in the deepest snow he could find. The Viscount Sotherby walked with their family. George took Mabel's arm through his and Mr. Badcombe was surrounded by Muriel and Susan, Harvey and Jane. Sir Albert Hagley walked a little behind them with Rachel. Aunt Catherine was between Uncle Harry and Cousin Aubrey. Lord Charles was talking with Wilfred. Uncle Sam and Uncle Ben were flanking the earl and his countess.

"Who usually helps you gather the greenery and drag in the Yule log, Randy?" Uncle Ben asked.

"Last year I was not here, sir," the earl said. "And for eight years before that Grenfell Park belonged to my cousin. I never came at Christmas time. In my grandparents' day I believe it was the servants' job to decorate the house.''

''Your cousin lived here and you never came?'' Uncle Sam said with a frown. ''How big is your family, lad, and where are the rest of them this year? Was there no one but your cousin and yourself?''

''I have several uncles and aunts and cousins,'' the earl said. ''We have never been close, I am afraid.''

''Amazing,'' Uncle Sam said, and he looked across to his brother. ''Isn't it amazing, Ben, eh? No family gatherings? No noise and confusion and insults. Just peace and quiet and being private. Do you think you would like it, eh?''

''Peace and quiet with Eunice?'' Uncle Ben said. ''I like family gatherings to get away from all the chatter, Sam.''

''Oh, Uncle Ben!'' Eleanor scolded.

''Oh, Uncle Ben,'' he said, imitating her tone. ''So the servants decorated, did they, Randy? And took half the fun of Christmas away from you. And did they eat the pudding and drink the wassail and sing the carols and kiss beneath the mistletoe as well?''

The earl smiled. ''Christmas has always been a quiet time with my family and me,'' he said. ''Very little different from any other day of the year except perhaps a little more depressing.''

''Depressing? Christmas?'' Uncle Sam's voice was a boom. ''The two words don't go together, lad. Not in a million years. Do they now, Ellie? But of course you have Ellie this year to make very sure that they don't. Eh, lass? You make sure that you whisk away a little sprig of the mistletoe when we get back to the house to hang above your bed. It does wonders for banishing Christmas depression. Is she blushing, Ben, eh? You are closer than I. Is she blushing, eh?''

''I think she is,'' Uncle Ben said, ''though it's hidden under the rosiness of the cold. Is Randy blushing, though, Sam? That's more to the point.''

''I hate to put an end to this delightful exchange of

wit," the earl said, "but we have reached the parting of the ways."

And to Eleanor's intense relief, he unlinked his arm from hers and called for everyone's attention. The pine trees and the holly bushes were to the east of the house, the heavier trees, including the oaks and the mistletoe, to the north. Soon several of the men, including her own husband, were trudging off north to haul in a Yule log, with a few of the girls to gather mistletoe. She went east with everyone else to find the holly and to pull down some pine boughs.

And found Wilfred at her side just when she was trying to recover from the embarrassment of being advised, in her husband's hearing, to hang mistletoe over her bed. She smiled at him and lengthened her stride so that Aunt Catherine and Uncle Harry would not get too far ahead.

"Ellie," he said, his voice low, his eyes directly on her, "how are you?"

They had always sought each other out, even before they had realized that they loved each other. Until now it had always seemed right to do so. He was very tall—taller than her husband. She had always liked the way her head barely topped his shoulder. His height had always made her feel small and feminine.

"I am well," she said, smiling brightly at him. "And you, Wilfred? You must be very excited about your partnership. Tell me all about it."

"Not very," he said. "It all somehow seems rather pointless now."

"Oh." She laughed. "It must be just that you are not used to your new elevated status yet, Wilfred. Cousin Aubrey must be very proud of you."

"How does he treat you, Ellie?" he asked. "I will not ask if you are happy. But does he at least treat you kindly?"

"But of course," she said with another laugh as they approached the pine trees and she remembered how just last summer they had eyes for no one else but each other, how they had held hands whenever they

were out of sight of others, and how they had stolen
kisses whenever they could. Just last summer. Just a
few months before. A lifetime before.

And then they were at the trees and Uncle Harry
was organizing them so that the men broke the boughs
they wanted from the trees and the ladies dragged them
away and heaped them ready for carrying back home.
There was much talk and laughter, much hard work.
Eleanor, doing her part, watched the Viscount Sotherby smile at Muriel as he handed a bough down to
her, and saw from the corner of an eye George and
Mabel exchange a brief kiss behind the screen of another bough.

She too might have been stealing glances and kisses,
she thought, if the events of the past two months could
just be erased. If Papa were still alive. If he had not
arranged a marriage between her and the Earl of Falloden. If . . . If and if.

Her husband had never really known Christmas, she
thought. He must have been a lonely child and boy.
Christmas had always been just like any other day of
the year to him except perhaps a little more depressing. He had a family to whom he had never been
close. None of them was at Grenfell Park for this
Christmas, while all of her family were. Except Papa.
She had not really thought of it until this moment. He
had four friends with him but no family at all.

She was swept suddenly by a wave of sadness and
longing. But a nameless longing. She could not quite
identify its source. She bent to pick out a few smaller,
lighter boughs for Davie and Jenny to drag home
through the snow and was quite unaware of the burning glances that Wilfred was sending her way.

Sir Albert Hagley had not intended to join the party
gathering greenery. He had come to Grenfell Park for
the shooting and he took it unkindly in the other guests
to have changed Randolph's mind. Not that he blamed
his friend, of course. The Transomes were an over-
powering lot, to say the least. And then his mood had

taken another turn for the worse when he had emerged from a solitary breakfast room and a solitary breakfast to encounter what seemed like several dozen noisy snowmen all pouring in from the outdoors, the Earl of Falloden leading the way, and he realized that he had missed a snowball fight.

Something as undignified as a snowball fight. And Miss Rachel Transome was there with the pack of them, joking and laughing with Harvey Gullis, who was not even a relative of hers if he had got all the relationships straight the evening before, and looking rosy-cheeked and bright-eyed and wet and untidy and altogether as appetizing a little female as he had ever clapped eyes on.

He had been planning to avoid her today. She might be an innkeeper's daughter and pretty and sensible, and she might have eyes for him as he had for her. But the truth was that the innkeeper was there with her and must weigh fifteen stone if he weighed an ounce. And there were plenty of other relatives there too to defend her honor. Besides, she was a guest in Randolph's house and a relative of his by marriage. And besides again, he had learned a lesson about women of a lower class from a certain Miss Eleanor Transome, now the Countess of Falloden.

He had planned to give Miss Rachel Transome a wide berth for that day anyway. For if he could not flirt with her and attempt some sort of seduction, his attentions might be interpreted another way and he might find himself leg-shackled to an innkeeper's daughter sooner than he could wink.

But she smiled at him as she shook her hood free from her damp hair. And she blushed, though he realized later that her cheeks had been rosy from the outdoors and if she had been blushing beneath it all he could not have known it anyway.

The upshot of it all, however, was that he found himself hunting greenery with everyone after all. His excuse to himself was that he could not be the lone male left at the house with the attic-raiding aunts.

Doubtless they would have him peering onto cobwebby rafters if he did anything so unwise. He went hunting mistletoe instead.

And of course he walked with Rachel Transome and talked with her and got himself lost among the oaks with her and only realized their lone, unchaperoned state as he descended the trunk of a gnarled oak tree to place some sprigs of mistletoe in her outstretched hand.

And because they were alone, and because she smiled so brightly up at him, and because he was an utter idiot who could not avoid trouble even when his mother and his sisters were not there to push him into it, he kept one small sprig in his hand and raised it above both their heads as he reached the ground and kissed her soft, cool lips.

Lord, he thought, withdrawing his head after the merest touch of temptation and smiling foolishly at the girl. Lord, he should have stayed away. He should have joined his own family for the holiday. He should not have taken pity on Randolph and come to give him moral support with this unspeakably *strange* family. Strange, noisy, boisterous, warm family.

"What do you do at your father's inn?" he asked her. He pictured her in a mobcap, a feather duster in one hand. He pictured male lodgers pinching her bottom and would have liked to line up all those customers so that he might walk along in front of them all, bashing heads together in pairs.

"I don't," she said, smiling. "We live in a house next door to the main inn. Papa owns several, you know. I help Mama with the running of the house. Twice a week I help teach school. Sometimes life is a little dull." She pulled a face.

Well. So much for the mobcap image.

"We had better find the others," he said, and she walked beside him, her mistletoe clutched in both hands, and they exchanged stories of school and university. She had attended school. Latin and history had been her favorite subjects. Cricket had been his. They laughed merrily.

He hoped fervently that they would not emerge from the trees to find Mr. Benjamin Transome waving a marriage contract before his nose. But the man, of course, was helping haul in the Yule log. When Sir Albert thought of the probable size of the log, though, he was not much consoled.

But by damn she was a pretty little thing. And sensible and good-humored. And now that it was too late, he wished he had lingered for just a few seconds longer over his enjoyment of her lips.

9

It had been a somewhat exhausting day. There had
been the early business of the morning and the snowball fight—all seeming as if they must have happened
days ago. And then the long trudge through the snow
out to the woods to bring home the Yule log and the
greenery. And luncheon followed by the loud and busy
decoration of the drawing room and dining room and
hall and stairway, a dozen voices at least giving firm
orders and a dozen more contradicting them. It was
amazing, the Earl of Falloden thought when it was all
over, that it had got done at all and that his house had
been so transformed. It looked warm and festive and
smelled wonderful.

There was the kissing bough, the proud creation of
Aunt Ruth and Jane Gullis, in the center of the drawing room, and sprigs of mistletoe in all sorts of unexpected places so that the most unlikely couples were
suddenly finding themselves stranded beneath some
while a chorus of voices crowed with delight and demanded a kiss. His wife and Hagley, for example, who
had looked startled and uncomfortable enough when
they had almost collided in the drawing room doorway
and who had both turned a bright pink when they had
been forced to peck each other on the lips. And Sotherby and Muriel Weekes at the pianoforte bench,
though the earl had a suspicion that perhaps that one
was more contrived—as the encounter between George
Gullis and Muriel's sister at the foot of the staircase
certainly was.

And as if they had not expended enough energy by

the time evening came, they all decided by mutual consent—it was frequently difficult with the Transomes, the earl was finding, to discover just who made an initial suggestion—to play a vigorous and highly competitive game of charades. The earl was surprised to find that he had some skill at the game—which he joined in despite the fact that he *never* played charades and despite the fact that he felt somehow as if his home and his life had been taken over by some alien horde, especially when cheered on by an enthusiastic team, which attributed its resounding victory to his acting abilities.

He was feeling rather pleased with the day and was beginning to wonder if there was not after all something to the fuss other people always seemed to make over Christmas. And his wife was looking rosy and cheerful and lovely. They had not once quarreled all day, he thought, though of course they had not been alone together all day either. He remembered suddenly the teasing of her uncles about the mistletoe over her bed and felt a not altogether unpleasant quickening of his breathing.

He was feeling relaxed, he realized in some surprise. Surrounded by Transomes, not quite master in his own home, not at all sure that he and his friends would ever get out to do some shooting, he nevertheless was feeling—happy. Was it a suitable word to describe his mood? Was he feeling happy?

Eleanor was not feeling at all as happy as she was at pains to look. Wilfred had hardly moved from her side all day, and apart from the misery his proximity was causing her, there was the fear that someone was going to notice. Her husband, for example. Everyone else must have known that they had not been indifferent to each other for the past year and more even though they had never shown their affection in public.

He had walked beside her on the way home with the pine boughs, and he had contrived to be the one handing her the ribbons and bows to be twined among the holly wrapped about the banisters on the staircase. He had been part of her team at charades. And now, when tea had been ordered, he had tried to maneuver her to the pianoforte to find a piece of music that had been played the evening before. There was a sprig of mistletoe hanging over the pianoforte.

She could stand no more, she decided. She was ready to burst with the tension of having her husband and the man who was to have been her husband in the same room together.

"We must talk," she murmured to Wilfred, and she raised her voice to tell those within earshot, her husband included, that she was taking him down to the library to choose a book to take to bed with him. It seemed an unexceptionable excuse, she thought. George and Mabel had already made an excuse to go downstairs to the long gallery—not to look at the paintings, but to gaze out at the snow and stars. But George and Mabel were all but betrothed, of course, and no one made any objection, though Aunt Beryl told Mabel to be back in half an hour.

Eleanor set down the branch of candles she had brought with her on the library desk and turned determinedly to face Wilfred. She wished he had shut the door, but she did not want to walk around him to do it herself. Besides, it was perhaps as well that the door remained ajar. There were servants whose good opinion was important to her.

"Ellie," he said, striding toward her.

But she set up a staying hand. "Don't come any closer, Wilfred," she said. "Please."

"How can I stay back?" he asked, nevertheless stopping and looking at her, longing in his eyes. "Ellie. My love."

"I am not your love," she said firmly. "Not any longer. I am a married lady, Wilfred."

"But you do not love him," he said. "You did it for your father's sake, Ellie. I know you have always despised members of the peerage and of the *ton*."

"Nevertheless," she said, "he is my husband."

"Ellie." He took another step toward her and stretched out both hands to her.

She looked at them and clasped her own more tightly in front of her. They were cold. She felt cold to the heart. He looked very tall and lean and boyish, though he was only two years younger than her husband, she reminded herself. "If you had written back to say you would marry me even though you had nothing much to offer me," she said, "I would have argued further with Papa. I would have stayed firm, if need be, until I came of age, though I do not believe Papa would have held out against me. He loved me. Or if you had written to ask me to wait for you until you could offer more and retain your pride, I would have waited. For five years. For ten. For however long it would have taken. You wrote to tell me that you must set me free. You wrote to tell me to do what Papa wanted me to do."

"You must know," he said, "how wretched I felt, Ellie, knowing the marriage your father had planned for you and having so little to offer you myself. You must know that I had to make the noble gesture."

"And yet," she said, looking at him with eyes full of hurt, "you came here, Wilfred. Was that noble? And you wrote that letter after Papa died and after I was already married. Was that noble? Why did you come?" She desperately wanted there to be a good reason, though there could be none. She was not accustomed to thinking of Wilfred as anything less than perfect.

"How could I stay away?" he asked. "Ellie, it is an agony to see you, to see him, to know that you belong to him. Oh, how could I stay away?"

"Perhaps for my sake," she said. "Did you think of what it would do to me, Wilfred, to see you here? To remember? And to know how fate played us such a wretched trick? Oh, Wilfred, did you not know of the coming partnership? Did you not suspect? You could have retained your pride and married me after all. But it is too late. Oh, I wish you had not come."

He took another step closer. "You know you do not mean that," he said. "You know you still love me. Let me hold you, Ellie. Just once."

"I am married," she said.

"But not by your own choice." His voice was urgent. "Tell me you love him, Ellie, or care for him at least. Tell me that and I will leave here tonight. I swear it. You don't love him, do you?"

"You know I do not," she said, "I married him because Papa was so set on it and because he was so very close to death and because there seemed no point in hurting him when you had written that you would not marry me. But my feelings for him have nothing to say to anything, Wilfred. The point is that I consented to marry him and did marry him and can no longer indulge my love for you. You must understand that. Oh, please, you must. You must not continue to look at me as you have been looking all day. You should not have come. Oh, I wish you had not come. I cannot bear it."

"Ellie." His voice was a groan. "I love you. It was only love that induced me to set you free. I thought I had nothing to offer you. But I was wrong. Nothing matters more than our love. And by now I would have had a great deal besides to offer you."

"All I ever wanted," she said softly, "was your heart. I never wanted riches or position. Especially not position." Her voice was shaking. She fought tears—she could not go back upstairs with red eyes. "Go," she said. "Please go. I should not have come down here with you after all. I must be alone for a few minutes."

"Ellie," he said.

"Please," she said, and finally he turned abruptly and left the room.

She whirled around to face the desk and leaned her arms on it. She closed her eyes and drew a few steadying breaths. He did not seem to understand that everything had changed, that no matter how they might regret decisions they had made in the past two months, there was no going back now to change matters. She blamed him for coming. And for writing that love letter. And yet she did not want to blame him. She wanted to find excuses for him. But what did he want of her? A clandestine affair? Did he not understand that she was married and that her marriage vows were sacred and quite unbreakable? Did he not know her after all?

She turned from the desk finally, her gaze on the floor. If she did not go back upstairs soon, someone was going to come looking for her. She straightened her shoulders and lifted her head.

Her husband was standing in the open doorway, one shoulder leaning against the doorframe, his arms folded across his chest. She stood still and looked at him as he stepped inside and shut the door firmly behind him.

He stood and looked at her for a long while. She was pale, but she was not crying. And she was looking steadily back at him. Of course, she would scorn to lower her eyes.

"Well, my lady," he said at last.

"I assume you heard all," she said. "Eavesdroppers rarely hear good about themselves."

"I did not even suspect that there might be need to eavesdrop," he said. "He is your cousin. I followed you down to help him choose a book, since I am more familiar with the library than you. But he did not need one, did he? He left here empty-handed."

"No," she said, "he did not need a book. But you have nothing to accuse me of, my lord. If you heard all, you will know that."

"It seems," he said, "that I was not the only one to give up a previous attachment to make this marriage."

"No," she said.

"And it seems," he said, "that you married me only because you thought your cousin would not have you and because your father was dying and you wished to please him."

''Yes.''

''Not because you wanted to be a countess and a member of the *ton?*''

She looked at him scornfully. ''You would naturally assume that,'' she said. ''There would seem to you to be no higher pinnacle to which a woman could aspire. I prefer real people, my lord. I prefer people who work to achieve what they want to those who live off the work of others and then squander their wealth on riotous and irresponsible living.''

''As I did,'' he said, ''to get myself so deeply into debt.''

''Yes.''

''Well.'' He looked at her broodingly. ''Things are not always what they seem to be. I could enlighten you, but frankly I have no wish to do so at the moment.''

You know I do not, she had said when her cousin had asked her if she loved her husband. Those words and the scornful tone in which she had spoken them were echoing in his head. And he felt wounded by them. Foolishly hurt. He had known that. There had been no pretense of either love or affection on either side. Quite the contrary. And yet her words had hurt him. Perhaps because they had been spoken to someone else? Because someone else now knew the emptiness of their marriage?

All I ever wanted was your heart, she had told her cousin, her voice soft and wistful. Those words compounded the hurt. She loved Wilfred Ellis but had firmly spurned his advances. Her behavior had been commendable. Perhaps he wished it had not been. He had no cause for fury and yet he needed the outlet of anger.

''Don't just look at me like that,'' she said, raising her chin. ''Either say something or let me go.''

''It seems we are not on an equal footing after all,'' he said. ''We did not have equally base reasons for marrying.''

She said nothing.

"And I suppose," he said, "that this family gathering, this merry Christmas that you are all enjoying so greatly, was deliberately planned to show me how very little you need me."

"You told me I might invite guests of my own," she said.

"You really do not have any great need for me, do you?" he said. "Your father left you almost half his fortune, and you have family members who would be only too happy to take you in."

"If you think to rid yourself of me so easily, my lord," she said, "you will be sadly disappointed. You are under no compulsion to live with me, I suppose, since you have several homes. But you are obliged to house and to provide for me. I will not leave you. Do not expect it of me or hope for it. According to the morality of my class, the marriage vow is taken for life."

"Apparently Mr. Wilfred Ellis does not know that," he said.

"I cannot answer for Wilfred," she said. "Only for myself. I am the troublesome little something that came along with what you really wanted when you married me. The money can be quickly and easily spent. I do not doubt that you will be as penniless and as hopelessly in debt after one year as you were two months ago. But there will still be me, my lord. You must accustom yourself to the fact."

"I intend to," he said. "We had better go back upstairs to the drawing room before all our guests wonder what has befallen us."

"Oh," she said, "doubtless they will think that we have stolen a few minutes to be together. I would not worry about our reputations, my lord. We are newlyweds, after all." Her voice was bitingly sarcastic.

"And so we are," he said, walking toward her. "It would be a pity to disappoint them, would it not? They should be able to look at you when you return and see all their happy suspicions confirmed. You should have a just-kissed look."

He stopped when he was close to her, set a hand behind her neck, and lowered his mouth to hers. She stood like a marble statue, though he persisted for a while, moving parted lips over hers, trying to soften them and force some response. Her eyes, he saw when he opened his, were not closed.

"You will live with me," he said, raising his head, "as long as I do not touch you? Is that the way it is? As it was with your father? *Don't touch me? Don't hug me?*"

"My father was in pain," she said. "It hurt him to be touched. But I have no right to refuse your touch. I made no objection, my lord."

He laughed. "Beyond schooling every muscle to rigidity," he said. "You are my wife, as you have just been at pains to remind me. Much as we both may wish that it were not so, reluctant as we both may be to continue what we both freely started, it is so. And by God, you will be my wife, my lady, from this day on. Expect me tonight in your chamber and every night henceforth."

"Yes, my lord," she said.

She had a way of being totally submissive and yet of sounding and looking so thoroughly aloof that she seemed like an impregnable fortress. He might have her body, she told him beyond the medium of words, but she would not allow him to touch any other part of her being. Her heart and her soul belonged to her and he would never be permitted a glimpse into either.

He felt chilled, and he wanted suddenly to get back upstairs, where there were people and gaiety and the beginnings of Christmas. Where there was the illusion of warmth and family and even love. *Her* family.

He made her a formal bow and extended an arm to her. "Shall we rejoin our guests?"

"If you wish, my lord." She set her arm lightly on his. "And if you have changed your mind about giving me that just-kissed look."

"I shall leave that for later, in the privacy of our

own apartments," he said, his voice as cold as her own.

And he realized for the first time consciously what had been happening to him in the last few days and even weeks. He had wanted to make something of their marriage, he had decided, because it had seemed the sensible thing to do in light of the fact that he was honor bound to spend a year with her. And yet inclination had had as much to do with his decision as good sense. He had wanted her, had begun to find her attractive. And not just physically. He had seen, especially since her family's arrival, that she was capable of warmth and laughter and spontaneity.

Well, so much for good sense and inclination. She had married him because her father wanted it and because the man she loved had refused to marry her. She hated the aristocracy in general and despised him in particular.

And the warmth and magic of Christmas, which perhaps he had come almost to believe in that day, were all illusion. It was no longer Christmas that was decorating his house but merely plants that would have to be taken down and somehow disposed of in a few days' time. And what were they doing anyway, celebrating Christmas with her father dead less than two months? Should they not still be in deepest mourning? He and she and her whole family?

They were singing again inside the drawing room, he could hear. Or some of them were. There were also voices talking and laughing. All the signs of high spirits that he had thought until half an hour before that he might perhaps after all enter into. But they were from a different world, her people. A world that was closed to him because of his background and upbringing. And because he had taken one of its members as his wife and destroyed her chances of happiness in so doing. Or had she destroyed his? He could not be sure which. Perhaps both.

He opened the door of the drawing room and stood aside to allow his wife to precede him inside.

* * *

She warmed her hands before the fire and stared into the flames and felt like crying. Not that she would cry, of course. She could not do so. She had been unable to cry since before Papa died. And she would not cry anyway when he would be coming into her room at any moment.

Christmas was going to escape her this year, she thought. Oh, it had seemed all day as if it was to be there with all the joy and wonder and magic that it usually offered. But it was not to be so. The decorations had failed to warm her heart on her return to the drawing room from the library, and the Christmas carols had failed to make her remember Bethlehem and a stable and a child and the meaning of it all. She had suddenly, with a great stabbing of grief, missed her father—and wished that he had not made her promise to enjoy Christmas for him. How could one force one-self to enjoy Christmas?

Her family's teasing had failed to amuse her. Uncle Sam had wanted to know, in a voice that had drawn the attention of everyone in the room, where they had been, and the witticisms had flown from Uncle Sam to Uncle Ben to Uncle Harry, and Aunt Eunice and Aunt Irene had advised the two of them to take no notice, and Aunt Ruth and Muriel and Susan had blushed. And then Tom had noticed where she was standing and pointed out the fact to her husband, laughing.

So he had been forced to join her beneath the kissing bough and set his hands on her shoulders and kiss her on the lips, while the teasing and affectionate jokes had resumed and Aunt Ruth had blessed her soul.

Eleanor shivered. There was to be no happy Christmas after all. And yet she had promised Papa.

Quite by accident she had met Wilfred's eyes across the room when the kiss was over. He had not even been disguising the look of desperate unhappiness on his face.

And now her husband was coming to her, she

thought, shivering again. Because his pride had been hurt. Because he had realized that she had never wanted his precious title and was not groveling at his feet with gratitude. Because he felt the need to make her his possession and destroy her own pride.

But she did not want it like this. She had been fooling herself since their arrival in the country. Not imagining that he loved her or even felt any real affection for her—no, definitely nothing as fanciful as that. But hoping perhaps that there could be peace, respect, even a mild friendship between them. But that hope was all destroyed now because he had found out about her feelings for Wilfred.

Wilfred! But she could not spare thoughts for him now. She would not. She had married someone else and there was only her marriage now. There was no point in pining for a love that could never flourish again.

And then he was in her room, without even the courtesy of a knock. She turned from the fire to look at him. He was wearing only a nightshirt. He looked grim. Not as if he were coming into his wife's room to make love to her.

She should fight him again, she thought as he crossed the room to her. But she did not feel like fighting. She had done so on her wedding night only because she had been terrified. She was not terrified now. Only very depressed because she did not want it this way. Not in coldness and anger. She pushed a stray lock of hair back over her shoulder.

Say something, she begged as his hands reached out to undo the buttons of her nightgown. But her plea came from so deep inside herself that it did not even reach her eyes, into which he was looking. *Kiss me. Let there at least be some pretense of tenderness.* But he said nothing and she stood still and impassive as he pushed the nightgown off her shoulders and it fell all the way to the floor.

He stood and watched her, waiting perhaps for her to do what she had done on their wedding night. Perhaps he expected her to undress him. She stood still, making no attempt to cover herself with her hands or to move closer to him so that he would not see her.

"Lie down," he said, and she turned to the bed and did as she was told.

She stared up at him as he pulled his nightshirt over his head and dropped it to the floor. *Please*, she begged him. *Oh, please, not like this.* But what did she want? Warm words? From him? Tenderness? Why should there be tenderness between them? *But please*, she begged nevertheless as she stared impassively up.

He came down directly on top of her and pushed her thighs wide with his knees and came deep inside her. She inhaled sharply, but there was no pain. She stared past his head to the canopy of her bed. Dull gold silk, heavily pleated, a large gold rose in the center. The candlelight was shimmering off some of the pleats. She waited for him to start moving in her.

And then his face was between her line of vision and the canopy. He had lifted himself onto his elbows. She looked calmly into his eyes and begged him silently.

"This is what it means to be my wife, my lady— *Eleanor*," he said, saying her name from between his teeth. "It does not mean holding me on the fringes of your life while you continue the way you have always lived. It means this. Intimacy. Constant nightly intimacy. And daily too, perhaps, when we no longer have guests to entertain." *To cater to my pleasure.* He might as well have said those words too, though he did not. "Do you understand that?" He began to move in her, very slowly.

"Yes," she said. "I have always been here, my lord. Every night. And every day. I have never denied you."

"You are denying me now," he said. "The marble statue, as you were earlier in the library. But it will no longer suffice to hold me off, Eleanor. From now ours will be a real marriage whether you like it or not."

"I like it," she said, and she could feel anger rising to her rescue to push back the dreadful depression that had made her so lethargic. She slid her feet up the bed on either side of his legs so that her knees were bent, so that she could feel him more deeply inside her. And she lifted her arms from the bed and twined them about his waist. "Do you think I have wanted a marriage without this? How else am I to have children?"

He held still in her. "You want children?" he asked her, and for a moment there was a look in his eyes that turned her heart over.

"Of course I want children," she said scornfully. "Who else am I to love?"

The look was gone from his eyes almost as if she had slapped his face. "Who, indeed?" he said. "Well, then, it seems that I do not have to feel apologetic for asserting my rights. We can derive mutual satisfaction from our encounters."

"Yes," she said.

He lowered himself onto her again and set his head close beside hers, his face turned away from her, buried in her hair. He did not talk again or kiss her. She closed her eyes and kept her arms clasped about him and concentrated on what was happening between them. She was not terrified or in pain or in a frenzy as she had been the first time.

It was pleasant, she thought in some surprise after a while, after dryness had given place to wetness and heat. It was not at all painful and surprisingly not at all humiliating. It brought a pleasant sort of ache that surged into her breasts, tightening them, and made her want it to go on for a long time.

She tightened her hold on him and raised her knees until they hugged his hips. And she wished there was love, or affection at least. It was so very intimate, this joining of their bodies, and so very pleasurable. But there should be more. There should be whispered words and kisses and tender hands. There should be a union of selves as well as of bodies.

She held him and felt him and smelled the cologne he had worn that evening. But in the most intimate embrace of all with her husband, she felt suddenly lonely. And close to tears again.

"Please." She turned her head to press her cheek against his hair.

He lifted his head immediately and looked down into her face. "What is it?"

She shook her head. Had she spoken? Cried out? "Nothing."

"Am I hurting you?" he asked.

"No."

He watched her eyes as the pleasure to her body and the pain to her soul continued. "Eleanor," he whispered, "you are my wife."

"Yes." She did not know what he meant. An apology, perhaps? She did not think it was a reprimand. She liked being called Eleanor. No one had called her by her full name before. *Kiss me,* she begged him silently. *Please kiss me. Please, I need tenderness.*

And then he stilled in her and she felt the extra warmth of his seed deep within and he lowered his head to sigh against the side of her face.

She would be with child soon, she told herself, sliding her feet back down the bed and relaxing beneath his weight. Then nine months later she would have someone to hold and to kiss and to love. By next Christmas, perhaps. But that seemed an eternity away. Though, of course, there would be all the months of feeling life grow and move inside her. Life that he had put there and she had nurtured.

He rolled off her and pulled the blankets up over her shoulders. And he leaned across her to blow out the candles that burned on the table beside the bed. In the sudden darkness she could feel him settling beside her and realized in some astonishment that he was not going to return to his room immediately.

Her cheek was almost brushing his arm. She could feel the heat from it. And from the rest of his body. She felt warm and comfortable and relaxed from head to toe. She refused to think any further. Tomorrow she would think. She let herself slide into sleep.

10

Perhaps he could persuade some of the men to go shooting today, he thought, staring up at the darkened canopy above his head. The room was actually surprisingly light though not yet with daylight. He suspected that there must have been more snow during the night. And he remembered the snowball fight that had started the day before and smiled at how incongruous its gaiety and spontaneity had seemed on the terrace of Grenfell Park. And how delightful, though he had not admitted that to himself at the time.

Certainly his own friends would go shooting. That was why they had come. Perhaps George Gullis would care to go too, and Tom Transome. His mind touched on Wilfred Ellis and slid away again. There was a cloud of depression associated with that name.

He needed to get away from the house with his friends and perhaps just one or two of the other guests. He needed to touch sanity and normalcy again. He recalled hearing the evening before that his wife and some of the other ladies were going on a visit to the school and the rectory during the afternoon to make final arrangements for the children's concert. So when he was arriving home, she would be leaving. Perhaps it was as well that way. Perhaps that was how they would achieve peace in the future—keeping apart as much as possible. Until the year was over, of course, and they could live permanently apart. Somehow neither thought was particularly cheering.

He turned his head to look at his wife, who was asleep on her side, facing him. Except at night for

what remained of the year, he thought. He had resumed their marriage the night before and he intended
to visit her bed regularly from now on. It was enough
that they were estranged in every other way. He felt a
sudden and unexpected wave of sadness. There was so
much love and joy in her family, boisterous and almost
overwhelming though they were. He had never known
that kind of warmth and love. His grandmother would
have called it vulgar. But it was not that. It was something . . . desirable.

But he would never know it. He would never really
be a part of her family. She despised him and loved
someone else. And he? Well, he had not chosen her
and had found her cold and unappealing. Though he
could no longer call her either. Even so, the greatest
closeness he could expect them to achieve was the
physical union his marriage to her entitled him to in
bed.

It must be morning, he thought. He must get up or
at least return to his own room. He wanted her again.
But she was sleeping deeply and peacefully and he had
already given her a disturbed enough night. He had
woken her twice during the night in order to make love
to her again, or to assert his rights and make something normal of his marriage, as he had explained it
to himself each time.

And yet each time he had known that there was more
to it than that. And he was still not quite sure what.
Was it perhaps that he really wanted to make a marriage of it? Was it that he wanted the physical closeness to her in the hope that it would bring some
emotional closeness too?

Good Lord, no, he thought as his mind moved one
question further on. She was the cit's daughter he had
been forced into marrying. He deliberately remembered his first meeting with her. He deliberately
thought of Dorothea. And of Wilfred Ellis and what
he had inadvertently overheard in the library the night
before.

No, definitely not that, he thought. All he wanted

was some peace, some workable way to live through the next ten and a half months. At Grenfell he would have his duties to perform during the day and she would have hers. At night he would take pleasure from coupling with her and she would take pleasure from receiving his seed. It could be an amicable arrangement. Nothing more or less meaningful than that.

And when she had a child, she would have someone to love, he thought, remembering her words of the night before with a stab of pain—with the same pain he had felt when she had said them. Did she not have him to love? he had thought then. A foolish thought, as he had realized at the time and realized afresh now. She despised him as she despised his whole class. And he did not want her love.

He must get up. He turned his head to look at her again, and she stirred and opened her eyes, almost as if she had felt his on her. She looked bewildered.

"Oh," she said, "what time is it?"

"I have no idea," he said. "Close to morning, I would guess."

And because she was awake and looked sleepy and warm and rumpled and because she was his wife, he lifted the blankets away from her and moved across to take their place and loved her once more before covering her against the morning chill and swinging his legs over the side of the bed and feeling for his nightshirt.

He could feel her gaze following him from the room, though she said nothing.

The morning passed fairly quietly. Her husband had gone shooting with his four friends and Uncle Harry and Tom. The other men were in the billiard room. Bessie and Aunt Eunice had taken the children and two sleds out to the hills to take advantage of the fresh layer of snow that had fallen during the night. Eleanor spent an hour belowstairs, talking with the housekeeper, consulting the cook on the Christmas menu, enjoying the atmosphere of the large, warm kitchen and the spicy smells of baking that were already filling it.

It would be a day spent with the women, she told herself as she came back upstairs and joined aunts and cousins in the morning room. The men would doubtless be gone all day. She would perhaps not even see her husband until dinnertime. And then there would be whatever evening entertainment was decided upon—and the night again. He would come again. He had told her that she must expect him every night. Would he stay all night again? she wondered. He had taken her four times the night before. Four times! She felt a deep throbbing where he had been.

"Ellie, dear," Aunt Catherine was saying, "you are in a dream."

"What?" she said, staring at her aunt vacantly. "Oh, I am so sorry. I am a little tired. I did not sleep too much last night." And then she lowered her head to her embroidery, flushing with mortification.

"We were all remarking on the splendor of the house," Aunt Catherine said, "and you were not responding at all to the compliments."

"Oh." Eleanor laughed. "Thank you."

"And his lordship, Ellie," Aunt Ruth said. "I cannot bring myself to call him Randy no matter what Eunice says. He is a very courteous gentleman, dear."

Eleanor smiled at her.

"And so handsome, Ellie," Susan said. "Far more handsome than Wilfred. Oh!" She flushed and looked uneasily at her mother. "I'm sorry."

"You must be very happy, Ellie," Rachel said.

"Yes." Eleanor smiled again. "I am."

She tested the idea in her head and realized in some surprise that she was not entirely lying. Of course she was not exactly happy. How could she be with Wilfred in the house? And how could she be when she was married to a man she could not respect, a man who was a spendthrift and a gambler and a womanizer? Although, she thought, she did not have any evidence that he had been either gambling or reckless with his money since their marriage. Perhaps he had turned over a new leaf. Perhaps she should give him a chance to reform. He had given up his mistress, had he not? She felt a fresh twinge of pain as she thought of him doing with his mistress what he had done with her the night before—and doing it since his marriage. But he had given the woman up and begged her pardon.

Perhaps she should give him a chance, she thought. Perhaps she should give her marriage a chance since there was nothing she could now do to change the fact of the marriage. And perhaps there was another night like last night to look forward to. She liked being in bed with him. She liked what he did to her. And she felt guilty at the realization since there was nothing else between them except that, and that should not be good when divorced from tender feelings. Should it?

There was a burst of laughter. "She is in a dream again," Aunt Beryl said, clucking her tongue. "I have almost forgotten what it is like to be a new bride, Ellie. But it is good to see, dear. I was afraid that perhaps it had been an arranged match, knowing how ambitious Joseph always was for you, but I can see that it is more than that. We were asking how many people can be squeezed into the sleighs this afternoon."

"Oh," Eleanor said. "There are two sleighs. I have never seen them. I shall have to ask the servants."

"No need, dear," Aunt Catherine said, looking out of the window, near which she was sitting. "Here are the men returned from shooting already. We can ask your husband."

Already? Eleanor folded her embroidery and waited expectantly, wondering if they would come into the morning room. She caught Aunt Catherine's eye, and her aunt smiled and winked at her.

They did come in briefly, looking red-cheeked and tousled. Uncle Harry and Mr. Badcombe had had some success, apparently, but none of the others. They did not seem unduly disappointed.

"It is beautiful Christmas weather," Viscount Sotherby said, smiling about at all the ladies. "It is almost a sin to remain indoors."

"We will have our quota of fresh air this afternoon," Aunt Beryl told him. "We are going by sleigh into the village with Ellie."

"Then I will not taunt and tease any longer," the viscount said with a smile and a bow.

Eleanor had sought for and met her husband's eyes as soon as he walked into the room. Quite unexpectedly she felt a great churning inside, as if her heart or her stomach or both had done a complete somersault. She felt heat rise into her cheeks, though she was sitting quite far from the fire. It was hard to believe, looking at him now, dressed for the outdoors, amongst other people, that they had been so intimate just the night before—just that morning. His eyes burned back into hers.

She felt instant embarrassment. She lifted her chin and clamped her teeth together and stared back at him defiantly as if he had just said something insulting. He looked steadily at her for a moment longer and then turned away to smile and address some remark to her cousins.

"Who are 'we'?" Tom asked. "Are all the ladies going into the village? If so, count me in."

"And me too," Sir Albert said. "I need to do some shopping."

"Bessie said that you and she are building snowmen with the children this afternoon, Tom, dear," Aunt Ruth said.

"Ah," he said, and turned away to the door.

"Rachel and I are going with Ellie and Aunt Catherine and Aunt Beryl," Muriel said.

"I'll ride with you, Bertie," the viscount said, "it being quite unfair for you to have all the ladies to yourself."

Eleanor's eyes touched on her husband's again. "I shall visit the school with you, if I may, Eleanor," he said. "I should get to know the children of my tenants and laborers as well as their parents."

She nodded and felt . . . warmed. Warmed? By the knowledge that her husband was to spend the afternoon in company with her? And voluntarily?

"Ellie?" Rachel said several minutes later, after the men had left the room and when the ladies had dispersed to get ready for luncheon. They were climbing the stairs together.

"Yes?" Eleanor smiled at her cousin. "We have not had a chance to talk much together, have we, Rache? I thought perhaps you would be betrothed by Christmas. To Mr. Redding."

Rachel flushed. "I believe he has been several times on the verge of offering," she said. "But I always will him not to, Ellie. I like him, but I am not sure I want to be married to him."

"Oh," Eleanor said. "What a shame. I like him too. Is there anyone else?"

"N-no." Rachel took Eleanor's arm and drew her into her bedchamber. "Ellie, gentlemen do not often marry girls of our class, do they? In your case, it was just that Uncle Joe was wealthy and influential. And you are so lovely. But such a marriage is unusual, is it not?"

Eleanor looked more closely at her. "Who is he, Rache?" she asked, her heart sinking. "Don't tell me it is Sir Albert Hagley, who has been showing you particular attention. But it has been only two days. You are too sensible for that."

Rachel stared at her. "It is foolish, is it not?" she said. "And he ignored me yesterday afternoon and evening. And he said he would come this afternoon before he knew for certain that I would be going too. Yes, it is foolish. I merely wanted to ask you about him, Ellie, since he is his lordship's particular friend. Does he have a—a sweetheart?"

Eleanor closed her eyes. "He is a rake, Rache," she said. "Stay away from him." She was aware that she should have explained more gently, but Rachel was her favorite cousin.

"Oh," Rachel said, "oh, I see. I knew I was being

foolish. But it is said that rakes are very attractive men. I'll follow your advice, Ellie. I suppose too it is knowing that he is a gentleman that has turned my head. A baronet.'' She sighed. ''That should make no difference, should it? And it does not. But he is such fun to be with, Ellie.''

Eleanor nodded. ''Stay away from him,'' she said. ''Please, Rache? I don't want to see you hurt.''

''I'll stay away,'' Rachel said, smiling rather sadly.

And she would too, Eleanor thought in some relief. Rachel was a sensible girl.

Originally Eleanor had expected to make the afternoon journey into the village alone. It was a duty call in her position as Countess of Falloden, though it was also a pleasure call. If there was one thing she was going to enjoy about her new status, she had decided as soon as they had arrived in the country and received that unexpected and wonderful welcome, it was her ability to do things with and for her husband's people.

But she was not sorry to have company. She was squeezed into one of the sleighs with Muriel and Rachel, Sir Albert and Lord Sotherby riding alongside talking and laughing with them. Her two aunts were in the other sleigh ahead of them, her husband riding beside them and conversing with them. He looked thoroughly at ease and had them both laughing over something he had said. He was the perfect gentleman. She had to admit that. Whatever he might think about her family, he would treat them with courtesy for as long as they were his guests.

She felt a surge of pride in him. And pride that she belonged with him. They were not feelings to be explored, she thought. She would not explore them. She wanted to enjoy the afternoon. It was, as the viscount had said earlier, wonderful Christmas weather. And it was a wondrous Christmas season, she thought, burrowing her hands inside her muff and watching her breath curl up in a cloud above her head. The sounds of horses' hooves thudding on the snow mingled with the jingling of the harness bells and the squeaking of the sleighs' runners.

She continued to stare ahead, not participating in the conversation of her cousins and the two gentlemen. He was her husband, she thought, watching his straight back, his strong thighs spread on either side of his mount, his gloved hands light on the reins. Her husband. The man with whom she was to spend the rest of her life. The thought no longer brought the horror and revulsion it had at first—it was even hard now to remember those first days. It was something she had accepted, because she had had to accept it or face a life of dreadful unhappiness. It was a—challenge. Yes, that was what it was.

She turned her head and met Sir Albert's curious eyes. They both looked away immediately.

It was the last day of school for the children. They were all scrubbed and combed and excited because the countess was to come to listen to their reading. Their excitement and the corresponding anxiety of the schoolmistress increased tenfold when her ladyship appeared with two other older ladies and none other than the earl himself.

The older ladies were introduced and one bowed grandly while the other smiled in motherly fashion, and both seated themselves in the chairs hastily brought forward for them by Miss Brooks, the teacher. His lordship stood rather stiffly inside the door, his hands at his back, while her ladyship smiled about at all the children and began to walk between their benches, talking with each of them.

Miss Brooks felt instant consternation. This had not been planned at all. She had not prepared the children for talking with a countess. She had planned that her ladyship, who was to have come alone, would sit on the chair that had been arranged carefully on the dais while the children rose one by one and read a few carefully rehearsed sentences from their readers.

Miss Brooks cleared her throat and was aware at the

edges of her vision of the motionless figure of his lordship and the seated figures of the two ladies who were
guests at Grenfell Park.

The earl watched his wife. She seemed quite unaware of the correct protocol for such an occasion. She
was supposed to be playing the part of the grand lady,
haughty and remote, striking terror and admiration
into the hearts of the children and of Miss Brooks.
Just as he was playing the part of the grand lord,
standing motionless in the schoolroom, frowning about
him.

Except that it was not a voluntary part that he
played. It was a part that was so ingrained in him by
his upbringing that he seemed to have no control over
it. The children were visibly relaxing at his wife's unexpected promenade about the room, at her warm
smiles. But instead of feeling chagrin at her improper
behavior—his grandmother would surely turn over in
her grave—he felt an unexpected envy. And an equally
unexpected pride. And something else. She was beautiful and warm—had he ever thought of her as cold?—
and kind.

But Miss Brooks was looking as if she were about
to have an apoplexy. He strolled the few steps toward
her.

"You have been here since the summer, ma'am?"
he said. "The Reverend Blodell informed me at the
time that he considered you a worthy candidate for the
post, and I have heard nothing but good reports of
your work since then."

Miss Brooks' plain face glowed with the praise as
she sank into a stiff curtsy. "Thank you, my lord,"
she said. "I try my best, my lord."

He smiled at her. "You have prepared them to
read?" he asked. "Her ladyship will be ready to listen
to them soon. We are not upsetting your day's sched-
ule?"

"Oh, no, my lord," Miss Brooks hastened to assure
him. "We are honored, my lord. More than honored."

"Then perhaps you will not mind if we talk to the children for a while first," he said. "We will not be interrogating them on their lessons, ma'am. It is Christmas." He smiled reassuringly at her again.

Miss Brooks had feared just that. She almost visibly sagged with relief, and looked back at the earl with something akin to worship in her eyes.

And now he had no choice, the earl discovered, but to turn to the children and begin speaking with them, as his wife was still doing. He was almost terrified. What did one say to village children? How did she manage to look so relaxed and so much as if she were really enjoying herself?

"You are having a concert tomorrow?" he asked the first group of little boys his gaze landed on. A foolish question, considering the obviousness of the answer.

They nodded, saucer-eyed.

He smiled and searched in his mind for something else to say.

"But we don't 'ave a place," one little piping voice said.

The earl found the source of the voice and raised his eyebrows. "No place?" he said encouragingly.

"The schoolroom is too small for all their parents, my lord." It was his wife's voice, warm and concerned and a little amused. "They have all been telling me about it. And the church hall had to be closed during the summer because the roof leaks so badly."

"Yes," the earl said. "I gave directions to have it reroofed just a few days ago."

There was a cheer from some of the children. With your father's money, he told his wife with eyes that hardened slightly on hers. An automatic defense since he expected her to have the selfsame thought. But she was smiling.

"In the meantime," she said, "they must either have their concert here in hopelessly overcrowded conditions or else use the church, which is not at all suitable."

"Unless there is an alternative," he said.

"Oh, my lord"—Miss Brooks' voice was embarrassed—"the schoolroom will do very nicely. It is very wrong of you, children, to burden his lordship and her ladyship with such an insignificant problem."

"But it is not at all insignificant, ma'am," he said, turning to her. "And there surely is an alternative." He looked back at his wife. She was still smiling at him. She knew his thoughts. He was sure of it. Just as a husband and wife should know each other's thoughts. It was a strange, unreal moment.

"We have a houseful of guests, Miss Brooks," she said, "who would be very delighted to watch the children's concert. And yet they could not possibly all squeeze in here with the children's parents and grandparents. Do you not agree, Aunt Catherine? Aunt Beryl?"

"I am quite sure," Aunt Catherine said, "that we will all be thoroughly disappointed if we have to miss it."

"Then it is settled," the earl said. "The children must all take home with them the news that the concert tomorrow will be held at Grenfell Park. To start at four o'clock, shall we say?" He looked about him, his hands clasped at his back. "Is that an acceptable solution to the problem?"

"To be followed by a party," his wife said. "With games and lots of good food." She smiled again at the children.

Some of the children stared back at them open-mouthed. The rest cheered. Two little boys even threw themselves backward off their benches and caused considerable commotion while Miss Brooks stiffened and glared.

"That is enormously kind of you, my lord, my lady," she said. Through the power of her will, without the medium of words, she drew toward herself the attention of her errant pupils. "I believe an appropriate gesture of gratitude would be applause, children," she said, leading the way with a light and elegant clapping of her hands.

The children clapped with more enthusiasm. The earl smiled at his wife and realized that for the first time in their relationship—outside of bed—they had acted together as man and wife. Together, without any previous consultation, they had planned a concert and party at the house for the children and their parents. Something totally unheard of in the neighborhood. Something his cook might well resign over. Something he felt enormously pleased about for some unknown reason.

"Miss Brooks," his wife said. "I understand that you wish the children to read to me. What a delight that will be. Where do you wish me to be?"

Soon she was sitting on the dais and he was standing close to the door again. But she had behaved with infinite wisdom, he thought, if she had planned it, that was. For now the children were no longer taut with excitement but relaxed with it. Even Miss Brooks looked less brittle. And the children proceeded to stand one at a time and read while Eleanor leaned forward and smiled her encouragement.

"How wonderful you all are," she said when the last child had sat down. "And what splendid readers. I have not been so well entertained in a long while. Is your concert tomorrow to be as good?"

The children all laughed.

"I am so looking forward to it," she said, getting to her feet. "Is Christmas not the most wonderful time of the year?"

The children looked as if they were ready to sweep back into conversation, but Miss Brooks signaled to them and they all rose and sang two verses of "God Rest Ye, Merry Gentlemen," bellowing out the words with marvelous enthusiasm and total disregard for the meaning of what they sang.

Yes, Christmas really was wonderful, the earl thought in answer to his wife's question as he opened the schoolroom door to allow the ladies to precede him from the room and raised a hand in farewell to the children and their teacher.

"And now to the vicarage," he said, "to inform Mrs. Blodell of the new location for the concert? And to tell her about the party?"

"Yes," his wife said, taking his arm. "I am sure it will all be a load off her mind, my lord."

He looked down at her as she turned to say something to her aunts, and marveled that the glow had remained in her eyes even when she had looked at him and spoken to him.

11

The uncles were restless from having spent the whole day indoors. If he played any more billiards within the next week, Uncle Sam declared during dinner, he would be stooped over permanently and would not have to worry about becoming an old man.

"The children had fun sledding, you said, Bess?" Uncle Ben asked. "A long hill, was it, eh?"

"Altogether too long for my energy, Uncle," she replied. "There are actually several hills, but of course Davie insisted on the longest and steepest."

"That's my grandson," Uncle Sam said, laughing heartily. "How many sleds are there, lad?" He turned to the earl at the head of the table.

"Six," the earl said. "Though why so many or any at all for that matter, I cannot explain, since I am the only person I know of who ever used one. Until this morning, that is."

"Six!" Uncle Sam boomed in delight. "Enough that there will not have to be long queues. They will bear my weight, lad?"

"Oh, assuredly, sir," the earl said, his expression slightly incredulous.

"Splendid." Uncle Sam rubbed his hands together in a gesture curiously reminiscent of his dead brother's. "If they will bear me, they will bear anyone. Ben is a stone lighter than I am—a mere feather. I am not sure about Irene now."

"Oh, Samuel!" she protested, flushing.

"Oh, Uncle Sam!" all the cousins chorused.

And so it was settled without any more discussion

being deemed necessary that dinner would be followed by the trek out to the hills in the darkness and
cold and an hour or two of sledding down the hills.

Just like a pack of children, Eleanor thought, looking a little anxiously down the table to her husband
and about at his four friends. Indeed, they would
doubtless be a great deal more unruly than children.
Were her husband and his friends used to them all by
now? And was it a permanent disgust they felt at the
vulgarity of it all? Or had they learned tolerance?

Her husband was looking his usual courteous self.
Totally unreadable, in other words. She had no idea if
his only outburst against her family, on the day of their
arrival, reflected his true feelings or if he had merely
been responding to the needs of a quarrel on that occasion.

They had quarreled again on their return home from
the village. Oh, not quarreled exactly. They had had
words and she had been put in the wrong at the end
of it all, so that she still felt thoroughly cross. The
wonder of the afternoon had been spoiled.

"You do realize, I suppose," he had said as he conducted her upstairs to her room on their return, "that
you almost succeeded in giving Miss Brooks an apoplexy in the school by neglecting to behave as a grand
lady should?"

"And that is?" she had said, stiffening.

"You should have nodded graciously and unsmilingly," he had said, "and allowed yourself to be conducted to the dais without delay. And you should have
listened to the children read and stammer with shaking
voices and then graciously recommended that they
continue to work hard until they could read well."

She had felt furious with him for his insensitivity.
Oh, and to think that she had begun to relax and forget
that he was of that most despised class, the aristocracy!

"Well," she had said, lifting her chin, "what can
you expect from the daughter of a cit, my lord? The
daughter of a coal merchant? What can you expect but

vulgarity? Perhaps you should take me back to town where I can be more effectively hidden away from public view. Where I will have less chance of shaming you.''

He had opened the door into her dressing room and bowed to her. ''What a hedgehog you are,'' he had said softly. ''If you had let me finish, I was about to say that I was glad you broke with convention. You set the children at their ease so that they enjoyed the afternoon instead of merely being awed by it.''

But she had looked at him with suspicion. Praise from the Earl of Falloden? Or was it mere condescension again? *It was all right this time, dear, but do remember next time that thus and so is how it is to be done.* She had swept past him and closed the door behind her. And wondered if they had quarreled or if they had not.

And now her relatives were planning to go sledding en masse. The trouble was, she thought, that she was itching to go herself. She wanted to streak down the longest hill at fifty miles an hour, if such a speed were possible, and screech her lungs out. She was thoroughly oppressed again by the restraints being a grand lady was trying to impose on her. Gracious, she had never in her worst nightmare dreamed of becoming a countess.

She glared defiantly down the table at her husband. He caught her look and raised his eyebrows.

Hedgehog indeed, she thought, thoroughly out of charity with him. She would hedgehog him!

Aunt Beryl and Aunt Ruth and Cousin Aubrey remained at the house. The children were not told of the expedition since they needed to go to bed early in preparation for Christmas Eve, Bessie explained. Everyone else trekked out to the hills, warmly wrapped against the crisp cold of the evening, six of them dragging the sleds. Several others carried lanterns, though they were not strictly necessary. The night was bright with snow and moonlight and starlight.

"Perfect Christmas weather," George Gullis said, nevertheless using the chill as an excuse to set an arm about Mabel's shoulders.

"Perfect lovers' weather is what you mean, George, my lad," Uncle Sam called. But if he meant to embarrass the lovers, he was disappointed. They merely looked at each other and grinned, starlight reflected in their eyes.

"Ah," Uncle Harry said, stopping in his tracks when they drew close to the hills, "now this is what I call perfect. Hills for the reckless and hills for the chickenhearted."

"And plenty of sheltering trees," Aunt Catherine said. "How lovely they look with their branches loaded down with snow."

It really was a lovely area for children, Eleanor thought. Or for the Transomes, who were all children at heart. Including herself. Oh, she wanted to be first down the longest hill.

"Well," Aunt Irene said, pointing to the hill with the gentlest slope, "I am not ashamed to admit that I am in the ranks of the chickenhearted. Sam, take me down that one."

Harvey and Jane, meanwhile, and George and Mabel and Tom and Bessie were racing up various slopes, sled ropes in hand.

"Miss Weekes," Viscount Sotherby said, turning to Muriel, "are you game for the steepest one?"

"Follow us down if you dare, Jason," Sir Albert called with a grin. He was already striding up the slope with Rachel.

"Oh, bother," Eleanor said to no one in particular. "I wanted to be the first down."

"How about third?" a voice asked from behind her. "We will grab a sled as soon as someone is down."

She turned and smiled. But some of the joy went immediately from the evening. "Third it is then, Wilfred," she said. And she looked at his tall, slender figure and imagined how it might have been if events had only been different for the past several months. It might have been a magical evening—sledding down the hills, getting lost for a few minutes among the trees, strolling slowly back home while everyone else walked on ahead.

She waited for a pang of anguish. Or at least longing. But she could feel only annoyance that he had come, that he was there, a constant reminder of what might have been. And she could not push from her mind the disappointment that he was not after all perfect. He should not have written her that letter, he should not have come, and he should not be seeking her out at every opportunity. And it seemed that whenever she overheard him talking to someone else, he was talking about his new position as partner in his trading firm. Reminding her of how close they had come to that happily-ever-after ending they had dreamed of.

She had wanted to be first down the hill. With someone else. With . . . Well, it was only right that she be with her husband most of the time. She sought him with her eyes in the crowd and saw him looking up the slope to where Aunt Irene and Uncle Sam were preparing to push off. She frowned. Why would she want to sled with him? Doubtless he disapproved of this whole outing. She might as well enjoy herself with Wilfred.

Aunt Irene shrieked and Uncle Sam bellowed.

Mabel screamed.

Sir Albert Hagley whooped.

The children were at play, Eleanor thought, and she allowed Wilfred to grasp her hand a couple of minutes later, as soon as he had one of the sleds, and draw her up the hill, through the deeper snow to one side of the run. She drew in lungfuls of cool air and determinedly set herself to have fun.

They seemed disconcertingly high up when they reached the top and she turned to look down. But it was a delight not to be missed. She sat down eagerly at the front of the sled and waited for Wilfred to seat himself, his knees on either side of her hips, his arms holding the rope on either side of her shoulders. And warm breath, and lips kissing her cheek.

"Ellie," he murmured, "I wish we could slide down the other side of the hill and disappear and never reappear. Don't you?"

But she felt only anger. No desire at all. "I want to slide down this hill," she said, bending her face away from his.

"He was outside the library," Wilfred said. "Did he give you a rough time, Ellie?"

She shrieked loudly. "Let's go!" she yelled.

"Come on, Ellie, Wilf." Uncle Ben, toiling up the hill with Aunt Eunice, stopped to clap his hands and whistle.

And then they were zooming down the hill, cold air rushing against their faces and into their eyes, and certain disaster seeming inevitable. Eleanor shrieked in real earnest and laughed helplessly when they arrived at the bottom and slid to a halt right-side up and injury-free.

"Ellie." Wilfred caught at her wrist as she jumped to her feet, but she pulled away and glared at him.

"Leave me alone!" she hissed at him, surprising herself. "You did not want me when you might have had me, Wilfred. Well, now you cannot have me. And I will not do things by halves. I belong to Randolph"—her tongue almost tripped over the unfamiliar name—"by church and by law, and by inclination."

"Ah, Ellie." He looked at her in misery. "You have been seduced by rank and property after all. I would not have expected it of you."

"I have been seduced by *marriage*," she said. "He is my husband. Leave me alone, Wilfred."

And then he was grabbing her by the wrist and dragging her out of the path of a zooming sled. She came back to reality and looked about her in some horror to see if anyone had witnessed their row. She did not think anyone had unless her husband, who was turning away to look up a smaller slope, had seen. He was too far away to have heard. She pulled her arm free.

"Lord Charles," she called gaily to her husband's friend as he got up from the newly arrived sled, laughing and dusting himself off, "would you care to try that again? With me?"

Sir Albert Hagley had decided quite impetuously to go into the village that afternoon. And he had ridden beside the second sleigh, talking with all three ladies—though Lady Falloden was too preoccupied with looking at Randolph to hear a word he said—and admiring the one dark-haired little beauty. And feeling uneasy. He had studiously avoided her since the morning of the day before. He did not want to give anyone the impression that he was courting the girl.

Yet in the village he would have walked with her if she had not immediately linked arms with her cousin and then somehow—he was not at all sure how it had come about—ended up walking with Jason. It seemed that she was not pursuing him either, then. A reassuring although somehow depressing thought.

Perhaps the day spent away from her company had lowered his guard, made him less careful. However it was, he found himself walking with Rachel Transome out to the hills and chuckling over her amusing anecdotes of family skating parties and boating trips. The Transomes, it seemed, knew how to have fun. It made him think ruefully of how all was prim and proper with his mother and sisters and of how important to them was gossip about those who fell short of their standards.

When they reached the hills, he found himself grabbing a sled, although there were only six, taking Rachel by the hand, and scrambling with her up the deep snow beside the run that the children had made that morning. And whooping and laughing with her as they sledded down the hill faster than the speed of sound—or so he swore to her, hand over heart.

"What a bouncer!" she said, laughing merrily.

He did not think of changing partners at every run as everyone else seemed to be doing. And he did not

think of how his evening spent with her would appear.
He did not wonder why she showed no inclination to
leave him.

He was just having too grand a time. Randolph's in-
laws, he concluded yet again, certainly knew how to
enjoy themselves.

Then Timothy Badcombe accused them of having
more than their fair share of turns with the sleds, and
he offered to fight a duel with Tim, and Tim chose the
weapons—snowballs—and they pelted each other with
furious energy until both of them fell full-length in the
snow panting and laughing. But the sled was lost. Tim
bore it and young Jane Gullis triumphantly up the hill.

"Well," Sir Albert said to Rachel, "I suppose that
leaves us to amuse ourselves with a sedate walk.
Ma'am?" he bowed and offered his arm and she smiled
and took it.

And of course their footsteps skirted the trees and
then wandered among the closest ones and then led them
deeper into the wood. And of course eventually their
footsteps slowed and finally stopped altogether. And
of course there was a tree trunk against which she
might lean her back.

He cupped her face in his hands and looked down
into her eyes, lit faintly by the moonlight. "If you
wish me to return you to your family, say so now,"
he told her softly.

He heard her swallow. And he lowered his head and
kissed her lightly, as he had kissed her beneath the
sprig of mistletoe. Her face was cold, her mouth and
breath warm.

"Mm," he whispered. "Sweet."

"Are you a rake?" she whispered back.

He drew back from her, though he still held her face
in his hands. "Because I have brought you here without a chaperone?" he asked. "I mean you no harm,
Rachel. Believe me. Do you want me to take you
back?"

She stared at him for a few seconds and then shook
her head slightly.

So he kissed her again. More lingeringly. More deeply. And he moved his body against hers, feeling its slight and slender curves.

Lord. Oh, Lord! He had spent years avoiding just this sort of situation despite the efforts of his mother and sisters. But the thought barely formed in his mind. He would think of that later. Tomorrow he would avoid her again. But not tonight. Not now.

Her arms came about his waist and all thought fled for the space of a few minutes. Or hours, perhaps.

Aunt Eunice was cold. Yet when Uncle Ben suggested, with obvious reluctance, taking her back to the house, she would hear of no such thing. What? Leave all the fun behind? They must build a fire, then, Uncle Ben announced, and the idea caught flame long before the one they all proposed to build. Did anyone have a tinderbox? Mr. Badcombe did. And so suddenly most of the revelers, the sleds and the slopes forgotten for the moment, were rushing among the trees to collect firewood.

Eleanor was one of them. But she went alone, ducking out of sight when she saw Wilfred looking about for her. Her husband was up on one of the lower slopes with Susan, who had been too nervous to do anything but stand at the foot of the hills for most of the evening.

Eleanor picked up a few sticks and twigs, shaking them free of snow, stepping a little farther among the trees to find more. And then she stopped and looked about her cautiously. The sounds were low, almost imperceptible. Certainly they were not the noises of people looking for firewood.

Rachel was standing with her back to a tree trunk, Sir Albert Hagley pressing her against it. They were in such deep embrace that they seemed quite unaware of her approach. They were both making quiet sounds of appreciation.

Eleanor froze in her tracks for a few moments before withdrawing backward as slowly and as quietly as she could. It was only when she had put some distance between herself and them and had turned to hurry out into the open that she thought that perhaps she should have made a sound, broken them apart, accompanied Rachel back to the others.

But Rachel! After the talk they had had just that morning. How could she? And with Sir Albert Hagley! The man who despised cits, the man who thought their only use was to be seduced if they happened to be young and female. Rachel was an innkeeper's daughter.

But in Rachel's defense, of course, was the fact that Sir Albert was a practiced rake and had two more years of experience than he had had when he had tried to seduce her.

She looked about her in panicked uncertainty. Uncle Ben? Should she tell him? Or Aunt Eunice? But there would be a terrible to-do. Everyone's evening would be ruined. Perhaps Christmas would be ruined. Perhaps Uncle Ben would feel it necessary to leave altogether. Or perhaps Sir Albert would be asked to leave. And perhaps Rachel, not realizing from what she had been saved, would never speak to her again.

Oh, Rachel!

And then she saw her husband beside the fire that was being built and he was turning and smiling at her.

"Are you going to bring them here, Eleanor?" he asked. "Or are you going to have your own fire over there?"

She looked down at the small bundle of twigs clutched in her arms and hurried over to drop them onto the pile. She caught at his arm.

"Please," she said, "I must speak with you."

He walked away from the group with her and looked down at her searchingly. "What is it?" he asked.

"It is Sir Albert," she said. "He has Rachel among the trees and is kissing her."

He raised his eyebrows. "One can hardly blame him for taking advantage of a perfect situation," he said.

"They have favored each other since they set eyes on each other."

"But," she said urgently, "he is a—a rake."

"Bertie?" he said in some surprise. "I think that is rather a strong word, Eleanor. Certainly I don't think he is about to ravish the girl among the trees with so many of her relatives close by."

"But he will have no respect for her," she said. "She is an innkeeper's daughter."

His eyes turned cold. "Oh, that," he said. "Yes, we members of the aristocracy all despise people of a lower class and waste no time ravishing their women if we have an opportunity. Or marrying them for their money, of course."

"Please." She caught at his arm again. "I know what I am talking about. From personal experience."

He looked at her blankly and then his eyes blazed. "Has he tried anything with you?" he asked, his voice tight with fury.

"Yes," she said. But she tightened her hold on his arm as he looked toward the trees and took one step away from her. "No. Not now. Not since our marriage. Two years ago. We were at a party in the country together and I knew by the way he looked at me that he liked me. But then I found out that he thought I would be of easy virtue because of who I was. He tried to—to touch me, and when he knew that he could not have me, he started sneering and calling me a cit. And soon everyone was calling me that and I had to spend the whole month fighting back. Rachel was allowing him to touch her. She does not know what he is like."

He was looking intently at her, his jaw set, his face still showing fury. "So you *were* the one," he said more to himself than to her. And then he relaxed somewhat. "He will not harm her, Eleanor," he said. "He is my guest, as is she, and they are very close to crowds of other people. It is a stolen kiss, nothing else. But tomorrow I'll have a word with him. I promise."

She felt the tension draining out of her. He was right. Of course he was. Rachel would be safe for that evening anyway. And tomorrow her husband would talk with Sir Albert, explain that Rachel was her cousin and his guest. Sir Albert would then feel honor bound to act the gentleman for the remainder of his stay at Grenfell Park. That was one thing to be said in favor of gentlemen. Honor was more important to them than almost anything else in life.

"Does it take twenty people or thereabouts to light one fire?" her husband asked her, turning to glance over his shoulder.

"It does," she said, "when they are Transomes."

Her answer won a grin from him, the first she could remember him directing at her. It made him look boyish and very handsome. It made her turn slightly weak at the knees.

"Look, Eleanor," he said, "six abandoned sleds. Shall we take one of them?"

"Oh, yes." She looked up at him eagerly. She had ridden down hills with almost every man present except him. "Do let's. The longest hill. It has been used so many times that it is marvelously slippery and dangerous."

"Which makes it marvelously irresistible," he said, taking one of her hands in his and the rope of one of the sleds in the other.

"Did you do this all the time when you were a boy?" she asked as they trudged upward.

"Not often," he said. "There was never anyone to slide with. It is not nearly as much fun doing this sort of thing alone."

"You were a lonely child," she said, looking up at him. "I was an only child too, but never lonely because there were always cousins."

"And your aunts and uncles to swell the numbers of the children," he said.

She looked at him sharply. But he was smiling, not sneering. "And Papa," she said. "He was always there too. Before his illness he had a great deal of energy and loved fun. You saw him only when he was close to death.''

But mention of her father only reminded them both of facts they wished for the moment to forget. The reason for their marriage. The bitterness they had both brought to that marriage. A silence—an uncomfortable silence—fell between them as he positioned the sled at the top of the steepest run. He straightened up and looked into her eyes.

''He always wanted what was best for me,'' she said. ''He thought this would be best for me. That was his only reason.''

But his lips tightened and he still said nothing. He waited for her to seat herself at the front of the sled and then lowered himself into position behind her, his legs and arms cradling her. She leaned back against his chest and wished that she had not mentioned her father. She wished that he would do what Wilfred had done earlier and kiss her cheek. But he was arranging the rope in his hands.

''A confession,'' he said. ''I have not been on this particular run yet this evening. It looks alarmingly steep, does it not?''

She smiled. ''If you wish,'' she said, ''I will follow you over to the smallest run. If you think you will feel safer, that is.''

For answer he lowered one boot to the snow and pushed them off. But perhaps his response to her taunt had been a little too violent. Or perhaps it was just that the runners of numerous sleds had made the slope far slicker than it had been earlier. Or perhaps it was that she turned her head to smile right into his face. Or the fact that he had pushed off with only one foot instead of two.

Perhaps there was no one single reason. And certainly they had no time to analyze it anyway. The sled was out of control from the first moment, swaying from side to side as he tried to hold it steady, gathering speed to a quite alarming degree, catching soft snow at an awkward angle halfway down, lifting into the air sideways, and pitching its cargo headlong into deep snow.

Eleanor had been too frightened even to shriek. But when she landed—on top of her husband, his arms locked about her—she found that they were both laughing helplessly. Giggling might be an apter word for what she was doing, she thought, but she was powerless to stop herself or produce a more dignified sound.

"Who wants to count arms and legs?" he asked when he could. "Do we have four of each between us?"

"Oh, I think so," she said breathlessly. "But I dare not count fingers and toes. You see? I told you we should be on the smallest run. It is for novices like yourself. We might have avoided disaster." She resumed her giggling.

"Disaster?" He had his own laughter under control. "Who said anything about disaster? I maneuvered that sled with consummate skill. Did you think I meant to take you to the bottom?"

She lifted her head and looked down into his face. And somehow forgot to giggle. And forgot even to breathe for a moment.

"Did you?" he whispered to her.

"Yes." She swallowed awkwardly.

"I meant to have us tossed into this deliciously cool feather bed," he said. "Quite out of sight of the fire gatherers, you see."

She could think of no answer to make. Not that she seemed to be called upon to say anything. His hand was at the back of her head, against her hood, and it was easier on her neck muscles to give in to its pressure and settle her mouth against his. And then she was glad she had done so. His lips were cool on hers, but his breath was warm against her cheek, and when his mouth opened over hers, it was warm too. And so was his tongue, sliding along the seam of her lips and then, when she opened her mouth, slipping inside. All the way deep inside.

There was none of the terror or revulsion that had set her to fighting blindly on her wedding night. Only warmth, beginning at her lips and spreading through her mouth and downward through her throat and her breasts and her womb until it throbbed *there* where he had been with her the night before. She wanted him there now. Inside her. Warm and hard and wonderful.

"Mmm," she said as his tongue withdrew from her mouth and he kissed her lips, her cheeks, her eyes.

"Mmm," he said, kissing her mouth again, darting inside with his tongue. "It is a very cool bed, is it not?"

He was lying full-length in the snow. She was on top of him. Even so, there was snow melting in uncomfortable places. And her feet were tingling with cold. She was lying on top of a man on an exposed hillside for all her relatives to see if they cared to step a few yards away from the fire, making an utter wanton of herself. For the moment it did not seem to matter that he was her husband. Ladies did not display open affection for their husbands.

She scrambled to her feet and began to brush away clinging snow. And since when did she care about what ladies did? She did not care. She glanced at him as he stood up beside her, lifted his greatcoat by the capes, and shook it.

"I'll wager," she said, "that you would not have maneuvered it so if you had had the fortune to marry a lady, my lord." What stupid, petulant words, she thought as she listened to herself almost as if she were a different person from the speaker. She could hardly blame him for looking at her in surprise. "I cannot imagine you rolling in the snow with Miss Dorothea Lovestone, for example."

He thought for a moment. "You are right," he said at last. "Dorothea would not even be out here. She would not so demean herself."

"There, you see?" she said, feeling even more childish because his tone was quite reasonable. He had not fired up at all. "She is a lady and I am not."

"Right," he said. "You are quite right. Dorothea, of course, has delicate health and would perhaps not even survive a roll in the snow. Another characteristic of ladies."

"While I am robust and not at all given to chills," she said.

He looked her over unhurriedly from head to toes. "Right again," he said, his voice maddeningly cool. She would have liked to pound her fists against his chest but would have felt foolish doing so. Where had been the provocation? All he had done was agree with her in the most amiable of manners. "But talking of chills, my feet seem to have changed places with two blocks of ice. Have yours?"

"Why should I have cold feet," she asked, "when I have none of the delicacy of a lady?"

"I would not know the answer," he said. "Let's go down to the fire, shall we?"

12

It had all started, he supposed, in the schoolroom when she had behaved so unconventionally and he had been neither embarrassed nor outraged, only a little envious and perhaps somewhat enchanted. And then there had been his reckless decision to have his home invaded by children and their parents on Christmas Eve, a decision made because of the brightness of her eyes and the smiling challenge in them. And her suggestion that the concert be followed by a party, an idea that had amused him when it should have appalled him.

That had been the start. Then, of course, there was her family—her loud, boisterous, fun-loving family, whom he would have considered unspeakably vulgar just a month before. The suggestion that they spend the evening out on the hills sledding—even the older generation—instead of engaging themselves with some genteel activity in the drawing room had shocked him at first. But then he had thought *why not?* Why ever not? It sounded like marvelous fun.

And he had been able to see that his wife, despite her demure behavior at the dinner table, was bursting with eagerness to get out there herself. She was a Transome to the very core. Strange, he thought, that he had not seen it in London. Or that she had not allowed him to see it.

Before they had left the house he had seen the spring in her step and the sparkle in her eyes that she could not hide. Out on the hills he had watched her race up slopes and shriek down slopes. Just as if she were nine years old instead of nineteen.

He had wanted to be with her. Yet good manners—those eternal good manners that were always opposed to simple enjoyment—had kept him with his guests. He had watched the quarrel with Wilfred Ellis and had guessed at what was being said. He had hoped, at least, that he was right. And he had rather liked the fact that Ellis might well be killing her love for him by his untimely persistence.

It was that thought that had brought into focus all that had been happening since the afternoon. Did it matter to him that her love for her cousin be killed? Whom did he want her to love? Himself? Habit at first drew a denial. But the Transomes were teaching him that habit was sometimes a dreary business.

He wanted to be with her. That was the simple truth of the matter. More than that he did not know—yet. And so he slid down a lower slope twice with Susan until she relaxed and admitted to finding it fun, and then strolled down to the site of the fire to find his wife.

Had their tumble into the snow been deliberate? He was not sure. But he was certain that it had been a very fortunate tumble. Very fortunate indeed. He had, he realized, been wanting to kiss her since he had not kissed her the night before. But she, of course, was not as ready for tenderness as he was beginning to believe that he was. After a brief but fiery response to his kiss she was her usual prickly self again. And on the defensive again, as she had been since he first met her. He had not realized it at first. He had thought her merely hostile.

"Let's go down to the fire, shall we?" he suggested.

He set an arm about her waist and they waded downward together until they reached the more packed snow that had been worn by many feet and found the going easier. She was looking thoroughly cross, he saw when he glanced down at her. She had wanted a good quarrel and he had denied it to her. But he did not feel like quarreling. He felt like laughing. He wisely held his peace.

"Anyway," she said as they approached the fire, which was now burning into glorious and incautious life—no sticks or twigs had been reserved for rebuilding it as it died down. It was a typical Transome fire, he thought with the new amusement that was still amazing and delighting him. "I think this is far more fun than wilting in a stuffy drawing room trying to look fragile and delicate."

"Do you?" he said. He would not give her the satisfaction of saying more. He almost chuckled aloud. He set her between him and the fire and set his arms about her waist and drew her back against him. Uncle Harry and Aunt Catherine were standing thus too, as were Tom and Bessie and George and Mabel. It was all highly improper, of course. One did not touch more than the hand of a lady in public, even if she was one's spouse.

Uncle Ben was talking about stars.

"You see, my theory is," he was saying, "that it must have taken them far longer than one night to reach that stable. They came from the East, the story says. How far east? One mile? Two? *Three* kings living just two miles down the road?"

"Have you ever noticed, though," Uncle Sam asked, "that the Bible never mentions three?"

"Well, then," Uncle Ben said, "twelve. *Twelve* kings living down the road? No, take my word for it, they came from a long way off and it took them longer than the one night."

"When I first married Ben," Aunt Eunice said, "I always used to wait for the inn to fill up at Christmas and then for two weary souls to come looking for a room. I used to picture exactly which stall in the stables I would put them in."

Uncle Ben chuckled. "You would never guess from looking at her that Eunice is a romantical soul, would you?" he said.

"She must be, Ben," Uncle Harry said. "I can't think of any other reason why she would have married you."

There was a merry burst of laughter.

"You walked into that one mouth first, Ben," Uncle Sam said. "You must confess."

"Yes, well," Uncle Ben said. "I was a handsome lad in my time. Anyway, back to the point here. The point is that that star must have been up there for longer than one night."

"And it comes back every year," Rachel said. She was standing beside Sir Albert, their shoulders almost touching. Both of them were rather dewy-eyed, the earl thought, looking at them critically. "That is what you always used to tell me, Papa."

"Right you are," he said. "It's up there now. The Christmas star. The Bethlehem star."

The group was strangely quiet, considering the fact that most of them were Transomes. They all gazed upward into the blackness beyond the firelight. Blackness and starlight. As if they expected that when they looked down again it would be to see a stable and a baby in a manger and shepherds and kings approaching.

"I think it is that one," Mabel said. But she spoke for George's ears only and turned her head so that he could kiss her briefly. Another highly improper gesture, the earl thought, resting his cheek against the top of his wife's head for a moment.

"That one," Aunt Eunice said. "It seems strange not to be at the inn for Christmas, Ben. Do you suppose John Pritchard is looking after everything for us?"

"The one close to the moon," Rachel said, and Sir Albert bent his head closer so that she could point out the star that seemed to her to be the brightest in the sky.

"That one," the Earl of Falloden murmured into his wife's ear. He pointed straight upward so that she had to lay her head back against his shoulder to see.

They gazed upward together into the wonder of Christmas and he felt it for the first time—that story of his faith that he had always celebrated at church in most sober fashion every Christmas.

"But it is right overhead," she said. "It should not be overhead until tomorrow night, should it?"

"Tomorrow it must be over the stable," he said. "Tonight it can be over us so that we can feel its brightness and warmth."

"I thought you never enjoyed Christmas," she said.

"I haven't," he said. "But then I have never gone looking for stars before." *And never with you before.* The words formed themselves in his mind, though he did not speak them aloud.

She laughed softly. "And is one to be found merely because one is looking for it?" she asked.

"But they are always there," he said. "Sometimes we just forget to lift up our eyes and look at them."

She let her head remain on his shoulder and gazed upward with him into a vast and mysterious universe that man so often forgot about, although it was always there and was always full of mystery and vastness.

My God, he thought, she was his wife. She belonged to him. She was his. For the first time in a long while he had someone who was his. His own family. His own to bring him comfort and companionship. His own to cherish and to love. My God! He was holding a treasure in his arms. What had her father said about treasures?

"The Bethlehem star is whichever star you want it to be," Uncle Ben said. "Whichever one leads you to peace and hope and love. Whichever one *feels* like the right star *is* the right star."

Uncle Sam chuckled. "He used to write poetry as a boy too," he said.

"Ah," Viscount Sotherby said. "But it is a lovely notion. It makes the Christmas story seem warmer and more personal."

"Then that is my Bethlehem star because I choose to make it so," the earl murmured warmly into his wife's ear. "Yours and mine."

She stood still against him, looking upward, her

head against his shoulder, saying nothing. It was a magical silence for a while, a silence during which he felt closer to her than he had ever felt to another person. A silence during which he could believe that they had become one because they were man and wife. A silence during which he fell all the way in love with her.

But there was not really silence. There were voices around the fire. And there was the crackling of the flames as they died down. His attention was distracted and the magic was gone. Perhaps she stood against him because he had put her there and she was an obedient wife. Perhaps she was silent because she had nothing to say. Or nothing that could be said in the hearing of her family. Perhaps she was as distant from him, as hostile to him, as she had ever been. He felt the chill that succeeded the heat of the fire.

"Anyway," he said, his voice its more cold and practical self again, "it is a pleasant, fanciful thought, is it not? And what is Christmas for unless for the indulgence of fancy?" He set firm hands on her shoulders and brought her upright and moved away with some of the other men to kick snow onto the dying flames.

"Piping hot chocolate back at the house for everyone?" he said cheerfully, raising his voice so that all could hear him. "And perhaps some brandy while it is being prepared? How does that sound?"

It sounded wonderful. Or so the loud chorus of voices assured him. And soon they were all trudging back to the house in merry groups of people who were, as usual, all trying to talk and all trying to make themselves heard by speaking one shade louder than the next person.

Eleanor, walking back to the house with her aunts and Bessie and Susan, felt cold and alone despite their cheerful chatter. And a little bewildered. Something—a nameless something—had been there within her grasp at the fire. She had leaned back against him and felt his broad shoulder beneath her head and his strong arms about her waist and known quite consciously that she was comfortable, even happy there. Even when she had thought of Wilfred and asked herself if she would be happier in his arms, she had been unable to feel any discontent.

He was her husband and somehow they were going to have to learn to live together. And during the course of the day it had come to seem a less impossible idea than it had at first. It had even begun to be a somewhat attractive idea. There had been that strange, smiling accord between them at the school. There had been his concern over Rachel and his promise to have a word with Sir Albert. There had been that kiss in the snow—her thoughts paused on that memory.

And there had been the fire and his arms and his shoulder and his voice. And the star he had picked out as his. And hers. Theirs. Their Bethlehem star, which was to lead them to hope and peace and love, according to Uncle Ben. She had believed it. Oh, she had been caught up completely in the unreality of the moment. She had believed it, and she had wanted it. With all her soul. With all her heart.

Then his voice again, quite matter-of-fact, telling her that it was a pleasant fantasy. She had been alone a moment later as he had helped put out the fire. She was alone now. Alone with her own foolishness. Only a little more than a month before he had married her, having set eyes on her only once, because he was in desperate need of money to pay off his debts and to enable him to live in the sort of luxury an earl must expect of life. She was of no importance to him. She was merely an encumbrance to him, and an embarrassment too. He had been ashamed of her behavior at the school that afternoon. Her cheeks burned with the humiliation of not having done there what she had been expected to do.

Not that she cared, she told herself. She had never wanted to be a lady. And never ever a countess. He had made her his countess because he had wanted Papa's money. Well, he had the money. And he had her too. He was just going to have to take her as she was. She would be damned before she would change just to please him.

There was hope. He kept telling himself that. He had to keep telling himself that. There must be hope. It was just that he must be patient. And not greedy. For he knew that he could never have all that he wanted. He could never touch the Bethlehem star even if it did appear directly over his head and even if he did reach out for it.

She could never love him. Not in the way he now dreamed of being loved. Their marriage had been made under too difficult circumstances. She had not wanted to marry him and had not wanted to enter his world. She loved someone else. No, it was unrealistic to believe that she could come to love him.

But there was hope. There was always hope. Certainly there was something he must tell her. There was a barrier between them and it was largely of his own making since he had considered it unimportant when he first married her to force the truth on her. He had disdained to do so. Now he wanted her to know the truth. It was important to him.

The Earl of Falloden left his bedchamber, tapped on the door leading to his wife's dressing room, and let himself in. She was there, seated before a looking glass, brushing her hair. It shone like copper.

"I believe our guests are enjoying themselves," he said, putting his hands on her shoulders as she set the brush down.

"Yes." She looked at him in the glass. "Even your friends. I think they are lonely gentlemen. Is that why you invited them?"

"I invited them and several others when I was foxed," he said, and wished he could recall the words even as he was speaking them. He did not add that he had been foxed because he had been unable to see a way out of marrying her. "I suppose these four accepted because they had nowhere else to go. Sotherby lost a wife in childbed two years ago. Did you know?"

"No," she said softly. She got to her feet and turned from the looking glass. "Poor gentleman. He is a kindly person. I like him."

She stood before him, making no attempt to move away. His hands reached up almost of their own volition to undo the buttons of her nightgown. She watched his hands. He felt a welling of desire for her. Of need for her. And not just a physical need. A need for *her*.

Steady, he told himself. *Have patience. Don't ever expect too much of her.*

"Eleanor," he said, opening the last button but pausing before pushing the garment off her shoulders, "I married you because of the money. I must admit that." Good Lord, he thought, could he have begun with more disastrous words? "But you have misjudged me even so," he said, rushing on, his voice stilted. He should have rehearsed this speech, got it just right before opening his mouth.

"Have I?" She raised her eyes to his. "Don't remind me of it. Please? Not at this moment. You want me in bed?"

"I am not a gamer," he said, "or unduly extravagant. Those debts were not mine."

"Oh, please," she said, as she lifted her hands and pushed her nightgown off her shoulders herself and shook it down her arms and over her breasts until it fell to her feet. She closed her eyes and walked against him. "I don't want to hear it. It does not matter. You are my husband and I have accepted that. Have I not? Did I not submit myself to you last night? Did I not please you?"

Acceptance. Submission. Her naked body pressed to his, her eyes closed submissively. Because she was his wife. Because she had agreed to marry him to please her father and would honor that commitment for the rest of her life. Duty and honor. She had no interest in hearing any explanations.

He turned a little cold. And yet he could feel her

soft, warm curves against him, his nightshirt the only barrier between them. He could see her breasts pressed against his chest and her dark red hair in shimmering waves over her shoulders and along her back. He desired her. He desired his wife and she would submit herself to him.

It was his heart that was cold. His body was on fire.

"I thought perhaps," he said, "you might be interested in knowing me. That perhaps we might learn to be friends."

"You want me in bed," she said, and her voice was as chilly as his heart. "Shall I go there?"

"Yes," he said, and he watched her walk through to the other room and lie down on the bed as he pulled off his nightshirt and dropped it to the floor with her nightgown.

He desired her, he thought as he looked down at her on the bed a few moments later, lying submissively on her back. He could feel the blood pulsing through him, and he needed to be in her. He needed to work toward release. He pushed her legs wide, knelt between them, positioned himself, and pushed inward. She was hot and wet. She wanted him too, then, for all the stillness of her body and the calmness of her face. They desired each other. He lowered his body onto hers and began to move swiftly and deeply.

And yet it was not the way he had wished it. His body worked feverishly toward its satisfaction while his mind remained strangely aloof. This was purely physical, he thought, wonderful as it was. This was merely his body taking pleasure from hers. The mere planting of his seed for her pleasure.

There should be something else. He wanted something else. He wanted to join their mouths as well as that other part of their bodies. He wanted to be able to look into her eyes and see her soul. He wanted her to gaze into his. He wanted words, words spoken and words heard. He wanted the Bethlehem star, he realized. And he knew that his own resolve to be content with less might not be enough.

He wanted her. Oh, God, he wanted her. Like this. Yes, like this and like this and like this. But more than this. He wanted more.

"Ah." He tensed in her and turned his face to sigh against the side of her head. And then he felt all the blessed relief of tension as he spilled into her. She lay still and quiet and soft and warm beneath him.

They were two very separate entities, he thought when thought returned to him. Two very different worlds. Joined in body as intimately as man could be joined to woman. His seed was in her, perhaps even the beginnings of their child. But worlds and universes apart. He uncoupled them with an ache of regret and moved to her side. Fantasy, he had called his feelings at the fire when he had wanted to defend himself against her silence. He had spoken the simple truth. It had all been fantasy.

He should go back to his own room, he thought. She had done her duty. Now he should give her rest. Tomorrow would be busy enough. And if he stayed, he would desire her again during the night. He should go.

He fell asleep.

And woke up some time later, a long time later—both the fire and the candles had burned themselves out. She was burrowing against him and muttering and searching for his mouth with her own. He knew she was still asleep even as he came awake and gave her what she sought. He kissed her hungrily with lips and teeth and tongue and wondered as she gradually woke up who it was she had been dreaming of. She was hot for whoever it was. Her breasts, he found when he pressed a palm against one, were tautly peaked.

But he would not think of the identity of her dream lover. He lifted her, warm and still sleepy, on top of him and drew her legs apart with his hands, bringing her knees up to hug his waist. And he lifted her by the hips and entered her as he brought her back down. He found her mouth again and loved her hotly and fiercely, as he had dreamed of loving her. And exulted in the growing heat of her and in the way she rode to his rhythm and tightened her muscles about him at the end until she cried out with him and shuddered down onto him as he drew the blankets up about her.

As she had done on their wedding night, he recalled. Except that there was a difference. Oh, there surely was a difference. She had been with him this time. All the way. Every step of the way.

"Eleanor," he whispered against her ear.

But she was asleep again.

Eleanor. My wife. My lover.

My love.

He resisted sleep for a while. He was too warm and comfortable and relaxed not to want to enjoy the sensations. And she was soft and warm on him. They were still joined.

My love. It was a wonderful dream. A Christmas dream. Perhaps reality would seem very cold in the morning. He wanted to stay awake and hold onto the dream.

He slept again.

13

Sir Albert Hagley was in the billiard room with Lord Charles, Aubrey Ellis, Wilfred, and Uncle Harry. The earl wandered in and watched for a while.

"Ouch!" he said quietly when Lord Charles, after making a couple of shots bordering on brilliance, missed an easy pocket. "A stroll in the long gallery, Bertie?"

Sir Albert opened his mouth to protest, looked into his host's face, and set his cue against the wall. "Why not?" he said. "It is too miserable to be outside. Snow and blowing snow—not at all kind Christmas Eve weather."

"It will clear by noon," Uncle Harry said cheerfully as the two men left the room.

"None of the ladies are strolling in the gallery," the earl said. "The lure of the fire in the morning room must be too tempting. We will have the gallery to ourselves."

"And is that important?" Sir Albert asked, looking curiously at his friend. "That we be alone, I mean?"

The earl did not answer. But he closed the door firmly behind him as they entered the gallery.

"Ugh!" Sir Albert said, strolling toward the nearest of the long windows that ran the length of one side of the room. "I hope Gullis is right about this clearing by noon. One hates to be housebound on Christmas Eve."

"What are your intentions toward Rachel Transome?" the earl asked quietly.

Sir Albert looked around in surprise. "My intentions?'' he asked. ''Good Lord, Randolph, you are not playing heavy-handed head of the family, are you? You aren't the head of the family. I imagine the butcher is—Uncle Sam.''

''You have been paying her a great deal of attention,'' the earl said. ''You were seen among the trees last night kissing her.''

''I would have been a damned slowtop if I had missed the opportunity,'' Sir Albert said. ''Have you had a good look at the girl? Or spent any time talking with her?''

''She is an innocent,'' the earl said. ''She is not up to your experience, Bertie. And she is an innkeeper's daughter.''

Sir Albert shrugged. ''Well, your wife is a coal merchant's daughter,'' he said. ''She appears to be fitting rather well into the role of countess. Are you warning me off, Randolph? I don't quite understand what this is all about.''

''I know your feelings about cits,'' the earl said.

Sir Albert stared at him. ''It was not so many weeks ago that you were damned deep in your cups because you were being trapped into marrying one,'' he said. ''Do you have such bitter regrets that you want to save me from making the same mistake? Do you find this family quite impossibly vulgar?''

''Rather the contrary,'' the earl said. ''I envy their exuberance and warmth and the affection they all seem to feel for one another. There have been moments when I have longed to be one of their number—and then I have remembered that I already am as Eleanor's husband.''

''Devil take it.'' Sir Albert looked at his friend with interest. ''You are growing fond of her, Randolph.''

But the earl's posture was stiff, his face unsmiling. ''She told me that you tried to seduce her at Hutchins' two summers ago,'' he said.

''Did she? So you know that it was her, then,'' Sir Albert said. ''I am not sure that seduction is quite the word, though, Randolph. I tried to take liberties, I suppose—see how far I could go. It was not very far at all.''

''Because she was a cit.'' The earl's voice was hard. ''You would not have treated Hutchins' daughter so, Bertie.''

Sir Albert was frowning again. ''Am I to answer for something that happened two years ago?'' he asked. ''Or rather, for something that did not happen?''

''I don't want it repeated with Rachel,'' the earl said. ''That's all, Bertie. She is my wife's cousin and my guest here. As far as anyone else is concerned, she is a lady and to be treated as such.''

''I would have kissed her last night if she had been ten times a lady,'' Sir Albert said. ''I am infatuated with her, if you must know, Randolph. Perhaps more. She has a deal more sense than most of the butterflies one meets in London ballrooms. And oceans more beauty. And I still maintain I am not answerable to you. I will answer to her father if I must.''

''Will you?'' The earl looked instantly relieved. ''You mean honorably, then, Bertie? Why did you say that Eleanor was vulgar?''

''I did not—''

''Yes, you did,'' the earl said. ''When you thought she might be the one who had been at Hutchins'. When I first talked of marrying her.''

''She *was* vulgar,'' Sir Albert said. ''Cockney accent that might have been cut with a knife. And loud, Randolph. And a laugh straight from the gutter.''

''Ah,'' the earl said. ''And was that before or after the attempted seduction, Bertie?''

''I did not notice it before,'' Sir Albert said, ''or I doubt I would have wanted to get close to her.''

The earl nodded. ''Ah, yes,'' he said, ''Eleanor would do that. I can almost picture it. Fists clenched, figuratively speaking, sleeves rolled to the elbows, and eyes flashing.''

''I have been having a hard time believing that she is the same woman, as a matter of fact,'' Sir Albert said. ''But listen, Randolph. I like this family. Who would not? They are making a rather cheerful time out of Christmas, aren't they? I have almost forgotten that I came here to shoot.''

''And you'll not harm Rachel?'' the earl asked.

Sir Albert looked at him somewhat uneasily. ''I have tried staying away from her,'' he said. ''At first, I suppose, because she is the daughter of an innkeeper and Mama would have a fit if I brought her up for inspection. Later because I did not want to find myself trapped in an impossible situation, with her whole family looking on and all that. I never did entertain the thought of seduction, Randolph. Good Lord, what do you think of me?''

''That you know how to behave,'' the earl said. ''But Eleanor was agitated. You really feel a fondness for the girl, Bertie?''

''Mama would have a fit,'' Sir Albert said.

''But you would be the one to have to live with the girl,'' the earl said.

''And so I would.'' Sir Albert scratched his head. ''Devil take it, it's quite a thought, isn't it? I had better stay away from her for the rest of today.''

''If you can,'' the earl said. ''I suppose you will discover the depth of your feeling in the course of the day.''

''Lord,'' Sir Albert said. ''An innkeeper's daughter. And a coal merchant's daughter. Does it matter, Randolph? I mean, does it really matter?''

''To me it does not,'' the earl said. ''And I had better go and see if Eleanor wants any help in the ballroom. She has decided that it should be decorated for the children's concert and party this afternoon.''

''I'll go back to the billiard room,'' Sir Albert said. But his friend did not step aside from the door when he approached. He stood and looked at him broodingly instead. Sir Albert raised his eyebrows.

''I'm sorry, Bertie,'' the earl said, ''but I have to do this. It is for my wife.''

And the next moment Sir Albert's expression turned first to surprise and then to pain as a fist connected sharply with his jaw. He staggered backward, stepped awkwardly, and went sprawling on the floor.

"If you want to make something of it," the earl said, "you can slap a glove in my face, Bertie. I'm sure we can both find seconds here and settle the matter well away from the house and the ladies."

Sir Albert flexed his jaw and felt it gingerly with the tips of two fingers. He frowned up from his sitting position on the floor.

"Growing fond of her!" he said in disgust. "You're bloody in love with her, Randolph. That's the first time—and the last, I hope—that I have been punished for a two-year-old crime."

"Do you want satisfaction?" the earl asked.

Sir Albert reached up a hand. "Help me up," he said. "It is the least you can do. Now I suppose I'll have a bruise to explain away to a couple of dozen curious people. I walked into a door. That is the easiest explanation, is it not? And the most humiliating. Devil take it, Randolph, when you throw a punch, you hold nothing back, do you? My head is going to be pounding for a month."

The earl hauled his friend to his feet and then extended his hand again in silence. Sir Albert looked at it and took it without another word. They left the gallery together.

Eleanor looked about her in some satisfaction. The ballroom, which she had thought a rather large, bare, cheerless room the first time she saw it, now looked festive enough for a ball. The children, she felt, would be delighted, and their parents too. She planned to be on hand to greet the parents when they began to arrive. She guessed that for some, if not all, coming to Grenfell Park would be as much ordeal as pleasure. She wanted to set them at their ease. She was, after all, plain Eleanor Transome, or had been until less than two months before.

She smiled as she watched her family doing much what she was doing, admiring their own handiwork.

Her husband had expected that she would set the servants to decorating. He had offered his help. It seemed he still did not know her family well. One word at luncheon and they had all set to with a will. Half of them had trudged outdoors, even though the storm had only just been dying down, to bring home more greenery. Aunt Beryl and Aunt Ruth had climbed up to the attic again to bring down the decorations that had not been used, though they both declared that there were not many left. Lord Sotherby had suggested going into the village to buy more ribbon, and Muriel, Mabel, and George had gone with him.

And then, of course, they had all decorated with enthusiasm. There was more than an hour left before anyone could be expected to arrive for the concert, an hour in which to wash and change.

"Well, Ellie," Uncle Sam said, sketching her an exaggeratedly elegant bow, "shall we waltz?"

She shook an imaginary fan before her face. "But Uncle," she said, "my card is full. I am so sorry."

They both chuckled and he set a comradely arm about her shoulders. "Happy, Ellie?" he asked.

She nodded. Her husband and Mr. Badcombe were holding the long ladder while Sir Albert Hagley, perched precariously on it high above them, was hanging stars from the chandeliers. All three of them were in their shirtsleeves. She doubted if any of the three had ever done anything like this before.

"He is a fine man, Ellie," her uncle said. "Joe chose well. Though if I know you, lass, you helped choose too. Love him, do you?"

She nodded. Yes, she did. She had realized it fully and consciously only the night before when she had woken to find him making love to her and had known somehow that she was making love to him too. Perhaps she had even started it. She had had the feeling that perhaps she had. But it had not mattered. They had loved. It had been the sexual act, the marriage act, the physical union of their bodies. But it had been far more than that. It had been what she had yearned for the night before without knowing quite what it was she wanted.

They had loved. There was no other way of describing what had happened. Physically it had been more than wonderful, for he had taken her beyond tensions and aches into a world of relaxation and peace whose existence she had never even suspected. Emotionally it had been—oh, there were not words to describe what it had been.

Yet today there was a certain flatness and uncertainty. She had woken early when he had turned her from her comfortable warm and living bed on top of him to set her on the mattress. And when he had withdrawn from her body with which he had still been coupled. But he had said nothing, though she had opened her eyes. He had only got up from the bed and turned back to tuck the blankets warmly up under her chin and to look for a lingering moment into her eyes. And today they had looked at each other and spoken to each other with amity, with none of the old coldness or hostility. But with nothing else.

Nothing to indicate that they had become lovers the night before, not just husband and wife engaged in the conjugal act. Perhaps she had imagined it? Perhaps he had not shared her feelings? Perhaps only she had made love.

"Yes," she said again. "I love him, Uncle Sam. I just wish Papa were here." And there was a pain and an emptiness suddenly, an ache in the back of her throat. Her father's absence from the ballroom, from their family gathering, was almost a tangible thing.

He squeezed her shoulder. "Me too, lass," he said.

Her husband was coming across the room toward them, smiling and brushing dust from his hands. "Rather splendid, would you not say, Uncle Sam?" he asked.

"What can I say, lad?" Uncle Sam said, releasing Eleanor's shoulder to spread his large hands expressively. "It has the Transome touch. Are you Ellie's next partner? She cannot dance with me, she says, because her card is full.''

"Is it?'' the earl said. "But she can hardly deny me, Uncle Sam. I am her husband. A waltz, is it?''

She laughed. "So Uncle Sam says,'' she said. "For myself, sir, I am having such a dizzyingly wonderful time at this ball that I hardly know which dances are coming up.'' She fluttered her eyelashes at him.

He took her hand in his and turned his head, looking about the loudly chattering crowed of her relatives until he saw the person he was searching for.

"Jason!'' he bellowed. "A waltz tune, if you please, on the pianoforte. You are the accompanist for this ball, are you not?''

Lord Sotherby looked at him blankly for a moment, his conversation with Aunt Catherine and Aunt Beryl interrupted. "Just taking a little break, my lord earl,'' he said. "I am on my way back to work, and a waltz it is.''

The sheer unexpected absurdity of it was its magic, Eleanor found over the next ten minutes as Lord Sotherby seated himself at the pianoforte and without the aid of sheet music began to play a waltz. Her husband bowed before her far more elegantly than Uncle Sam had done and extended a hand for hers.

"Ma'am,'' he said. "My dance, I believe?''

She consulted her imaginary card. "And so it is, my lord,'' she said, dropping into a deep curtsy.

Then they were waltzing, a dance she had never performed outside the schoolroom, and she would have sworn on a stack of Bibles that they were dancing on air. And she was smiling into his eyes and he into hers and there was a welling of happiness in her. He must have felt it too, then, the night before. It must have been mutual. Oh, it had never been like this between them.

"Quite a squeeze, is it not, ma'am?'' he said, and she looked about her to discover that almost everyone else was dancing too. Even Aunt Ruth was being twirled about by Mr. Badcombe and looking as if she might break into shrieks at any moment.

"Christmas," the earl said, laughing down at her. "It makes the sanest people mad, does it not? I daresay we will all return to sanity next week."

Was that all it was, then? Was it just Christmas? All of it? Would the magic go next week? Vanish without trace? Would there be no more friendship and teasing—no more imaginary balls—next week? No more lovings?

"I hope not," she said, and watched a light leap into his eyes for a moment before he looked away suddenly as the music came to an end.

The noise level in the ballroom increased tenfold and there was a great deal of laughter.

"We had better retire and get ready for this concert," the earl said, raising his voice and somehow making himself heard above the hubbub. "Those who wish to attend it, of course."

Everyone wished to attend it, and they all told him so in voices raised to be heard above those of their neighbors. The earl grinned.

Eleanor turned when a hand came to rest on her arm.

"Ma'am," Sir Albert Hagley said, "may I take five minutes of your time? May I speak with you?"

She would really rather not. She always felt a great deal of embarrassment in his presence and avoided him whenever she could. She had been under the impression that he shared her feelings.

"Of course," she said warily. "Shall we stroll into the conservatory?"

She led the way from the ballroom.

"The weather has improved," Sir Albert said, fingering the velvety leaf of a plant and strolling over to the windows, which made up three sides of the conservatory.

"Yes," she said. "I am so glad for the sake of the

children and their parents. And for our sakes. Now we will all be able to go to church this evening.''

There was an awkward little silence. Why had he asked to speak privately with her? she wondered. He was the last person she would have expected to do so.

''I owe you an apology, ma'am,'' he said abruptly, turning resolutely from the window and looking directly at her.

She returned his look with some surprise. He had done nothing to offend her. And unexpectedly she remembered how she had thought him attractive at first at Pamela's party—but only at first. He was rather slight of build, his face narrow, his eyes dark, his hair a mid-brown. She could understand why Rachel liked him. And Rachel had used the word *attractive* to describe him.

''At long last,'' he said. ''My behavior was unpardonable. Both at first and later. Sometimes the surest way to deflect the humiliation of rejection and the discomfort of guilt is to turn contemptuous. That is what I did, and I recall that I turned everyone else with me. It must have been a very distressing time for you.''

Good heavens, he was talking about what had happened two years ago. She felt herself flushing. ''Yes, it was,'' she said. ''Though I made certain that no one else knew it at the time.''

There was a dull flush on his face too. ''The cockney accent,'' he said. ''You do it well. And the loud laughter. I did not suspect that it was all an act, that in reality you are as refined as any l—. As any lady. You *are* a lady, ma'am.''

She was suspicious suddenly. ''Did my husband demand this apology?'' she asked.

''No,'' he said. ''Though he did bring the matter up this morning when he spoke with me about Miss Transome. Miss Rachel Transome.''

She bit her lower lip.

''You need not fear a repetition of what happened two years ago,'' he said. ''With your cousin, I mean. And I do sincerely beg your pardon for that, ma'am.

There should have been someone there at the time to give me a good thrashing.''

She smiled slowly. "Thank you," she said. "You are my husband's closest friend, are you not? I have wished that it were not so. I have felt all the awkwardness of having to be in company with you frequently."

"Yes," he said. "I have felt it too." He walked toward her and reached out his right hand. "Will you take my hand, ma'am? Can we be friends too?"

"I would like that," she said, setting her hand in his and returning the pressure of his handshake. Her eyes strayed to the bruise on the left side of his jaw and she remembered the merciless teasing he had had to parry at luncheon. "That door you ran into," she said. "Was it my husband's fist?"

He looked at her and pursed his lips.

"Because of Rachel?" she said. "Oh, but he should not have."

"Because of you," he said. "Because I did not show you the proper respect two years ago."

"Oh." One hand strayed to her mouth, but she could not stop it from smiling behind the hand. And she could not stop her eyes from dancing. "Oh," she said again.

"And you are pleased about it," he said, "even though my jaw still hurts like the very devil. Pleased that he hit me, ma'am? Or pleased that he cared enough to do so?"

The latter. Oh, the latter. "Sir Albert," she said, "I am so sorry about your poor jaw. But don't you think Christmas is a wonderful time of the year? Don't you?"

"I have had better days, I must admit," he said. "But I suppose this one might improve. There is still a good deal of it left. And may I say that for the first time I am glad that Randolph's cousin was the way he was?"

She looked at him in incomprehension.

He raised his eyebrows. "Because if he had not

been,'' he explained, ''then Randolph would not have met and married you. Did you not understand my meaning?''

''His cousin?'' she said, staring at him blankly. ''Have I missed something? What are you talking about, please?''

''His cousin, the former Earl of Falloden,'' he said. ''The devil of a dissipated apology for a man, if you will excuse my language, who beggared the estate and ran up debts so high—mostly from gaming—that everything would have been lost if he had not had the good fortune to die first. Randolph inherited the debts, though he might have repudiated the personal ones. Your father bought them all and the mortgage on Grenfell Park. You must have known. Didn't you? Oh, good Lord, what have I said now?''

She set a hasty hand on his arm. ''Yes, I did,'' she said. ''I knew about the debts and his reason for marrying me. Except that I assumed that the debts were all my husband's.''

''Randolph's?'' he said with a laugh. ''That is rather comical actually. When we were at university, and afterward too, he was the only one of the lot of us who always managed to live within his income, though it was probably one of the smallest. This is all new to you, is it? Perhaps I should have kept my mouth shut.''

''No.'' She looked up at him and smiled radiantly. ''No. Oh, thank you, my friend.'' And she bit her lip and continued to smile. He had tried to tell her the night before. She realized that instantly, though why he had not told her long ago she had no idea. But she had stopped him the night before. She had wanted to make love with him and she had not wanted her ardor to cool—it had been in danger of doing that as soon as he had reminded her that he had married her for money. In fact, it had done so. She remembered her passivity during their first loving—her refusal to show him that she wanted him, that she enjoyed what he did to her. Oh, she should have listened. She should have heard this from his own lips.

"I must get ready for the children," she said suddenly, turning to the door. "Are you going to watch their concert?"

"If I do not," he said, "it seems that I will have only myself for company. Yes, I shall watch them."

She linked her arm through his as he opened the door and they proceeded into the hall and up the stairs. "The day will get better," she said. "I promise. It is Christmas. Everything is new and wonderful at Christmas. No one is allowed to be unhappy at Christmas—even when nursing an aching jaw." She laughed and he smiled back at her.

When she reached her dressing room, she hummed to herself and performed a few waltz steps with an imaginary partner before ringing for her maid even though she knew that she must have scarcely half an hour in which to get ready. But she paused suddenly, her hand on the bell, arrested by a new thought.

Wilfred! She had not spared him a thought all day, even though she had set eyes on him a few times. She had not thought of him. Whereas she had thought a great deal about her husband. She had admitted to herself that she loved him. But she loved Wilfred—didn't she?

The answer was very obvious. No, she did not. He was not important to her any longer. Because she was fickle? *Was* she? Were her feelings so easily changed? But it was marriage that had changed her, she thought. The forced closeness and intimacy of marriage. It had made her see her husband's attractiveness—not just the attractiveness of his person but that of his character too. And she knew now from what Sir Albert had told her that she was not mistaken. He had married her for her father's money, yes. But it was to save the house and estate where he had grown up. She knew from the evidence of the past days that he loved Grenfell Park. He had not married her just out of the selfish desire to continue with an extravagant way of life.

She smiled softly and closed her eyes. She loved him. She tested the newness of the idea with her mind and whispered it to the room. Perhaps he did not care very deeply for her, though she believed that his feelings had certainly softened. Perhaps he would never love her. But she was not going to let that thought depress her. It was Christmas and anything and everything was possible at Christmas. She remembered promising her father that she would have a wonderful Christmas for him. She also remembered his saying that she would be glad one day for the marriage he had half forced her into.

Well, then.

She turned to smile at her maid as the door opened.

14

The Earl of Falloden entered his wife's dressing room to accompany her downstairs to the ballroom.

"We will greet people as they arrive," he said. In truth, he was not much looking forward to the afternoon after all. Something like this had never been done at Grenfell before and he did not know quite how to proceed. He was somewhat regretting his impulsive offer of the afternoon before.

"Oh, yes." She flashed him a bright smile. "They will be so happy, will they not, to be coming here. And the children will be so excited they will be feeling sick. I can remember when we used to perform Christmas pageants as children, my cousins and I. There was always that sick anticipation and then all the joy and triumph of having done it and of hearing the praise of the adults. They always praised us even if we forgot our lines or tripped over the hems of our costumes."

She was alight with excitement and would remain so through Christmas, he guessed. She was flushed and beautiful and looked hardly as old as her nineteen years. He envied the fact that she could look forward to such an ordeal with pleased excitement.

"Eleanor," he said, "don't expect everyone to be too glad. For most of the parents and grandparents it will be an awesome thing to come here and be greeted by us. Most of them will not enjoy the afternoon. But they will talk about it and remember it for the rest of their lives."

She looked at him incredulously. "What nonsense!" she said, laughing. "You may choose to play the part of stuffy earl, my lord, but I will not play stuffy countess.'' She was not trying to quarrel with him, he could see. She was smiling. Her eyes were dancing with merriment.

"You don't quite understand, do you?'' he said. "They are not parts we can choose or not choose to play. They are there. We are the Earl and Countess of Falloden. To these people we are great personages, to be treated with some awe.''

Her smile faltered. "Are you warning me?'' she asked. "That is it, is it not? You are reminding me who I have become so that I will not disgrace you by behaving with vulgar familiarity as I did at the school yesterday.''

Perhaps after all she was ready to quarrel. He reached out a hand and rubbed his knuckles along her jaw. "Hedgehog,'' he said. "Let's go down, or there will be no one to greet. And I like you very well as you are, Eleanor. I liked the way you were at the school yesterday.''

"You did?'' She looked at him uncertainly, warily. "It was not vulgar?''

"My grandmother might have called it so,'' he said. "I am not my grandmother.''

"Oh,'' she said, and took his arm.

People were going to be arriving at any moment, he thought, and felt foolishly apprehensive again. People he felt quite comfortable with out in the fields or in their cottages he dreaded meeting socially in his own ballroom. He would take refuge in his most stately manner, he supposed, and yet he did not want to behave that way. He wanted these people to be able to enjoy the concert and their children's performances.

Then he saw the Transomes. Though perhaps it was unfair to use that single name, he thought, when actually he saw Gullises and Weekeses as well as Jason and Charles and Tim. Yes, and Bertie too. There they all were, congregated close to the ballroom doors and all in their best party humor—which was just a little more exuberant than their usual humor. Uncle Sam was rubbing his hands together.

"This is quite like old times," he said, his voice booming even more loudly than it usually did. "Do you remember the Christmas pageants, Ellie? Your Aunt Irene was forever digging me in the ribs so that I would not laugh in the wrong places and wound you children's feelings."

"This is Christmas," Uncle Harry said, beaming around at everyone. "Children and concerts and parties. What else is Christmas all about? Bring on the next generation, I say. Tom is doing his part all right. It's your turn now, Ellie. And everyone else's duty to choose partners as soon as possible."

He chuckled as a chorus of "Oh, Uncle Harry!" came from the younger generation.

"Well, I'll be making an announcement along those lines later tonight—after midnight," he said with a wink for Aunt Beryl.

Mabel was blushing, the earl saw at a glance, and George was looking at her, thoroughly pleased with himself.

"On with the concert, I say," Uncle Ben exclaimed, "and bring on the party and the tea. This is Christmas and time to stuff stomachs to overflowing. What say you, Randy?"

The earl could feel his wife looking up at him. Her arm on his was somewhat tense, and her eyes were anxious, he saw when he looked down at her. A few days before he would have been a little shocked and definitely taken aback. Now he was merely amused.

"For myself, Uncle Ben," he said, "I intend to eat until my clothes are one stitch short of bursting at the seams."

Everyone chuckled, himself included. Though he sobered quickly. There were several people coming up the stairs and approaching the ballroom. All of them looked rather as if they were on the way to their own executions. He mentally adjusted his manner and smiled.

And then the Transomes—including all the extras who might as well have borne that name, judging from their behavior—greeted his guests. Oh, they were not so ill-mannered as to crowd him out and give him no chance to do so himself. He shook everyone by the hand and bade them welcome to his home. His wife at his side did the same, though she also assured several anxious mothers that yes, their children had arrived some time before and were in a salon with their teacher getting ready.

But it was the Transomes who pumped the hand of every new arrival and boomed out greetings and laughed and chattered and reminisced about Christmases past and assured everyone that this was the very highlight of the season's festivities and took everyone into the ballroom and seated them before the make-shift stage and sat among them to continue the conversations. And generally set all his guests so much at their ease that the noise level in the ballroom became almost deafening. As if there were a few hundred Transomes in there.

"Well," the earl said, looking down at his wife when it seemed that everyone had arrived and was seated, "so much for grandeur and awe."

"I am sorry," she said, "if the occasion has been spoiled for you. But I will not apologize for my family. They have helped everyone to relax."

"Including me," he said, and she looked up at him in some surprise. "How I envy your family, Eleanor. They have so much capacity for enjoying life. One loses so much when one thinks and behaves only as one ought. As one ought by the standards of some aristocratic killjoy, that is."

She smiled at him warmly, her eyes fully focused on his so that for a moment he forgot the roomful of noisy people just beyond the doors of the ballroom and smiled back at her.

"I am going to see if I can help Miss Brooks with the children," she said. "I would be willing to wager—if it were ladylike to wager, of course—that at least a dozen last-minute crises have arisen.''

"It is on the tip of my tongue to advise you to stay away," he said, "on the assumption that the sight of the countess will only intensify the crises and create a dozen new ones. But I am learning not to trust the tip of my tongue. Go, then.'' He almost added the words "my love" but stopped himself just in time. There was amity between them as they had agreed, first in London and then during the journey down to Grenfell. Perhaps there was a little more than amity. But he must make no assumptions about her feelings. He must not rush his fences.

He watched her hurry down the hallway to the small salon that was serving as a dressing room for the children. And he felt totally relaxed, he realized, and ready to enjoy the coming hour or two. All his dread and his fear of awkwardness had disappeared. Strange, he thought. He was learning a great deal from his countess about how to be an effective earl and landlord. When he had expected to have to be the teacher, he was in fact the pupil.

A cit's daughter. A coal merchant's daughter. Eleanor. His wife. His love. He smiled after her disappearing figure and turned toward the ballroom. The level of conversation dropped a little as he entered, and a few of his laborers looked as if they thought they might be expected to scramble to their feet. But he smiled and nodded about him and took a seat at the back and remembered Uncle Harry's words.

Yes, this was Christmas. Children and excitement and anticipation. And warmth and fellowship. How fortunate that Christmas had found him at last. How fortunate that Mr. Joseph Transome, needing to settle his affairs in a great hurry before his death, had fixed his attention on him when choosing a husband for his daughter.

He wished suddenly that Mr. Transome were still alive so that he could thank him.

Everyone had come, Eleanor assured the children. All were eagerly anticipating the concert. And no, of course they would not forget their lines or their steps in the dance. One never did when the big moment came. And if by chance—by some very strange chance—they did, then Miss Brooks would be ready to prompt them and all their parents would love them and feel proud anyway. And she was so looking forward to seeing their performances, she assured them. She could scarcely be more excited if she tried.

The children were still highly nervous when she left them and Miss Brooks looked taut enough to snap in two. But at least she seemed to have left them in a mood of nervous excitement rather than nervous dread. She smiled as she hurried back to the ballroom and remembered what Uncle Harry had said. It was her turn to produce children so that the next generation could perform Christmas pageants.

She hoped—oh, she hoped it would be soon. Two nights of lovings and it was the very middle of her month. Perhaps already . . . But she must not expect anything too soon. If she did, she would only be doomed to disappointment if nothing happened. She must have patience. And she must hope that her husband had meant what he said when he had told her that she must expect him nightly from now on. If not this month, then, next month or the month after. She so wanted to be with child. With *his* child.

She smiled brightly at everyone when she entered the ballroom, noted the lowered noise level, and responded to it.

"They are all ready," she said. "Now if they can just force their legs to obey their will, they will be here within a few minutes."

There was general laughter as she took the chair beside her husband's, smiled at him, and set her hand in his. Too late she realized that the last gesture was probably quite inappropriate. But she could not withdraw her hand without being conspicuous. His own had closed about it warmly and rested it against his thigh.

"Oh, my lord," she said, "I am so glad you suggested having the concert here."

"Are you?" he said. "And so am I."

But before she could wonder at this new warmth between them—in him as well as in her—Miss Brooks appeared in the doorway, followed by the children in silent single file. There was a sudden hush, Uncle Sam began clapping and everyone followed suit, and the children filed up onto the stage to sing their first pair of Christmas carols. Three or four voices sang sweetly in tune. The rest growled along somewhere in the base octaves of the pianoforte. Eleanor smiled and leaned forward in her seat.

There were choir renditions and solos and duets and recitations and dances. And finally the Christmas pageant itself, in which Miss Brooks had ingeniously devised speaking parts for every single child. Mary spoke in a whisper that probably even the baby Jesus could not hear; Joseph boomed out his lines in a voice that would have put even Uncle Sam to shame; the angel of the Lord forgot her lines, but the shepherds were so busy being sore afraid that Miss Brooks was able to prompt her quite unobtrusively; one shepherd brought his crook down on the bare toes of another shepherd and prompted lines that were not in the script, not to mention a little unrehearsed hopping on one foot; one king's turban fell down about his face as he knelt to lay frankincense at the foot of the manger and Mary had to help him readjust it; the heavenly host inexplicably consisted of the growlers rather than the singers.

But it was all wonderful. Not just because the performers were children and all their parents and grandparents were sitting and watching, fairly bursting with pride and amusement. Oh, not just because of that. But because however imperfectly reconstructed, it was the Christmas story. Jesus was born and all was wonder and awe and happiness. There was in the whole story not one whisper of the Easter that was to follow so soon after. Only the wonder of unconditional love come to earth in a newborn baby.

"Oh," Eleanor said, looking up at her husband after the children had all taken their bows and filed out of the ballroom, looking considerably more cheerful than they had when they came in. But she could think of no other words. Her hand, she saw, was still in his even though she must have released it several times in order to applaud.

He raised her hand to his lips. "I must go up there and remind everyone that all are invited to the party," he said. "Come with me, Eleanor."

She accompanied him onto the stage, their hands still clasped, and she smiled down at everyone as he spoke, praising their children and their teacher and inviting them all to stay for the children's games and the tea. She felt the response of her husband's people—the warmth and the affection. It was true, perhaps, that they would always be set somewhat apart, she and her husband. They could never make real friends of these people. Like it or not, she was a countess and he an earl. And maybe that was the way it should be. Her husband, after all, had a great deal of responsibility for their well-being. But warmth and affection were enough. They were far preferable to awe and distant respect.

The original idea had been to have games for the children and then tea for everyone. Of course, that idea did not take into account the fact that there would be Transomes present, all but two of them adults. But children to the very heart when it came to games.

When "Marching to Jerusalem" was announced, Uncle Sam took charge, arranging the chairs in a long line down the center of the ballroom, booming out instructions for the children to sit down, and announcing that there were at least a dozen chairs to spare. And so Eleanor took one and Uncle Ben another. George and Mabel joined in the game. Then a few of the less shy parents came to occupy still-empty chairs, egged on by their excited children. And a merry romp it was, the last adult falling out only when there was no other adult to roust but only children. A child must, of course, win each game.

And when it came to blindman's buff, Aunt Ruth declared that she had not played it for years and agreed to play it this time, provided Muriel joined her. That drew Viscount Sotherby into the game. Then Jane and Harvey joined in and at least a dozen of the village parents. And Eleanor, of course, who was unanimously chosen by shrieking children to be the first to have her eyes bandaged.

The party became truly that, with everyone either participating or smiling on from the sidelines and cheering relatives. Indeed, the Reverend Blodell declared to the earl, his lordship had shown great condescension this day and had earned the eternal gratitude of his people. The earl felt an unaccustomed itch to join in the games.

Then, while Mrs. Blodell was repeating to him her husband's speech but at far greater length, he found that he had no choice. Races had been organized and the third was to be a relay race, two adults and five children to each team.

"And we will have his lordship, the Earl of Fallo-den, to lead team number one," Uncle Sam was announcing in his customary roar, "and Sir Albert Hagley to lead number two, and . . ."

A relay race. Good Lord! And yet as he crossed the ballroom to join his team—the other adult was Eleanor just as the other adult on team number two was Rachel—he found that his people had been given the perfect opportunity to let off some feelings about him. There were whistles, cheers, jeers, catcalls. He grinned.

"How does one do this, anyway?" he asked his wife as all the other teams were forming up.

"You have to step inside a sack," she said, "and

hold it up while you jump the length of the ballroom and back. Then you pass the sack on to me.''

"Good Lord," he said incautiously.

She laughed merrily and was joined by the children on their team, who had been listening.

"It is easy, m'lord," one little boy said, "as long as you do not fall.''

"As long as I do not . . .'' The children shrieked with glee as he frowned. "And what do I do if I fall?''

But Uncle Sam was giving the order for the first member of each team to get ready to scramble inside his sack. "When I say 'Go!' '' he said.

The earl soon discovered what one did when one fell. One rolled and crawled and tried in vain to get back onto one's feet without entangling them in the folds of the sack. And one inspired loud jeers from the onlookers and agonized groans from one's team members. And one was invariably the last back for the changeover to the second person on the team. One also acquired a bruised elbow and an inability to stop laughing.

His wife did much better—the result of a lifetime of practice, he guessed—and caught up ground on the other ladies, most of whom either fell or moved rather slowly. His team was third going into the third round, second going into the fifth, and second at the end.

"Well," he said, laughing around at his team, "that was fun. And who cares about coming in first, eh? Second sounds good enough to me.''

A row of footmen appeared with trays of food and drink as their master was running a three-legged race with Aunt Catherine, and set them out on the tables that had been laid at one side of the ballroom. The race over, a somewhat disheveled and breathless earl announced that tea was ready and that his guests were invited to help themselves. He suggested that contrary to custom, the children be allowed to go first, and the tables were attacked by hot and cheering hordes. The lemonade and the cold fruit punch proved to be the most popular items at first.

And then somehow, just when the party might have been expected to come to a natural end, the dancing began. Country dances, vigorously executed by people who were more used to performing the steps on the village green or about a maypole. It was hard to know who had suggested it—it was not Uncle Sam this time. When Uncle Sam suggested something, one was left in no doubt of the fact. Miss Brooks was playing the pianoforte and a little later the viscount. And almost everyone joined in. There were sets of children and sets of young people and sets of older people.

Somewhere in the middle of all the country dances Lord Sotherby played a waltz, throwing most of the dancers into consternation until they watched the few couples who knew how to perform the steps and joined in after a few minutes, laughing and watching their feet. Even the children tried it.

The earl waltzed with his wife and wondered if there could be more exhilaration dancing with her even at a fashionable ball to the accompaniment of a full orchestra. Sometime they would try it, he thought. Sometime when it would no longer matter that she did not wear mourning and he could take her back to London. Not that he craved London and its amusements. He rather thought that he could be content at Grenfell for a lifetime if this amity—and perhaps something more—with his wife could only continue. If only they did not discover in a few days' time that it had all been Christmas and nothing else.

Bertie was dancing with Rachel, he saw, their heads bent together, talking. They had eyes for no one but each other. So much for Bertie's determination to stay away from the girl today. He wondered if Uncle Ben was expecting a declaration at any moment and if Bertie was still reluctant to be snared. But then, the two of them had known each other for only a few days. It could easily be construed as a Christmas flirtation and no more.

Except that there was a look about them both that suggested somehow more than just a flirtation.

Another hour passed before the music stopped and the punch bowls had been attacked again and everyone was leaving as if on a prearranged signal, all flushed and smiling and pouring out their gratitude to the earl and his countess, who were standing to one side of the doorway. It was the very best party anyone could remember, if several heartfelt assurances to that effect could be believed.

"A happy Christmas, my lord, my lady."

"A happy Christmas, Mr. and Mrs. Mallory. And—Michael, is it? You were a very convincing king in the play earlier."

The greetings went on and on until finally all the guests had left and Uncle Sam and a few of the cousins were gathering up sacks and scarves and other paraphernalia of the party games and Aunt Ruth was blessing her soul and saying that it was quite like old times, and how wonderful it was of his lordship and dear Ellie to give them such a splendid party. Just as if it had been arranged solely for their benefit.

"I did not like to say this while all the guests were filing past you," Uncle Harry said, smiling wickedly at the earl and his wife, "but do you realize where you are standing?"

That particular question at Christmastime could mean only one thing. The earl looked up and sure enough, there was the sprig of mistletoe he had fully expected to see there.

"Thank you, Uncle Harry," he said. "It would be a dreadful shame to waste it, would it not?"

And he took his wife into his arms and kissed her firmly and lingeringly while Transomes and their disciples cheered and whistled about them.

He did not believe, the earl thought as he raised his head and smiled down into his wife's eyes, that he had ever felt happier than he felt at that precise moment. And he had no wish at all to look beyond the moment.

"Happy Christmas, Eleanor," he said.

"Happy Christmas, m—, R—, Randolph," she said.

15

Dinner was late, the party having gone on longer than expected. But then as Uncle Ben said—and everyone agreed—they had stuffed themselves so full of good food at tea that things needed to settle for a while before they could do justice to dinner. And it would be a shame not to do justice to it when Grenfell's cook was such an excellent soul.

And so the interlude between dinner and having to leave for church was no longer than an hour. And almost before they could drink their tea and dream up some activity to fill in the hour, the carolers arrived from the village and congregated in the great hall with their rosy cheeks and their sheets of music and the snow melting on their boots.

The carolers, who always left the great house until last because it was the farthest distance to walk but always wished afterward that they had made it first because it was such a dismal ending to a happy evening, were in for a surprise. The former earl had always appeared on the staircase only when they had finished singing, and he had appeared only to nod stiffly and wish them the compliments of the season. The earl and countess before him had always come onto the staircase at the beginning and bowed and nodded graciously before instructing the servants to bring out refreshments, and then disappearing to their own apartments.

Not so with the new earl, whom some of the older singers remembered as a quiet and serious and rather wistful boy. The new earl appeared at the top of the

stairs, almost before they were all inside with the doors
closed behind them, his countess on his arm. And they
both came right down the stairs into the hall, followed
by all their guests, who it was said were a jolly lot,
most of them being the countess's relatives.

No sooner had the singers begun their first carol,
"The Holly and the Ivy," than some of those relatives
unexpectedly joined in. And before the first verse was
at an end, almost everyone was singing, including, the
carolers noticed to their astonishment, the earl himself.

Four carols were sung at each house on the carolers'
route. Sometimes at the big house they had stopped at
three. But on this occasion they would not have been
allowed to stop at four even if they had wanted to or
had thought of doing so. The hall rang to the sounds
of one Christmas carol after another, so that even the
two footmen on duty looked as if they might at any
moment break into song.

Eventually the earl gave the nod to have the wassail
bowl carried out and the bowl of hot cider and the
trays of warm mince pies. And yet after eating and
drinking, the carolers and the guests of the house and
the master and mistress too felt compelled to sing once
more before loud and seemingly endless greetings and
handshakes were exchanged and the carolers were
waved on their way from the open door just as if they
were not to be seen again at church within the hour.

There had been much animated discussion among
the women—no one thought to consult the earl or the
countess—about how everyone was to be conveyed to
church in two sleighs. They would just have to make
several trips, Aunt Beryl said. The men could ride, of
course, Aunt Eunice decided. And if they were prepared for a little discomfort, Aunt Ruth declared, they
could seat three in each sleigh.

Of course, the wait at church for those who went
first would be tedious. And those left behind would be
anxious that they would be late to church. But the
youngsters were quite capable of walking, the distance

being little more than a mile and the weather now clear and still again, as it had been the night before.

If it came to that, Aunt Beryl said, she was quite capable of walking the distance too. Indeed, Aunt Catherine added, the exercise would be good for them after all they had eaten in the last few hours. They had walked out to the hills the night before, Aunt Irene reminded them, without thinking about the distance, though they must be almost as far from the house as the church was. Well, if everyone else was prepared to walk, Aunt Ruth said bravely, no one must go to the trouble of calling out a sleigh just for her. She would walk too. Doubtless either Sam or Ben—or Aubrey for that matter—would be willing to take her on his arm if she tired. But she did not believe she would.

And so by the time the earl thought to mention that he had ordered the sleighs and both the carriages brought around in time to convey his guests to church, everything had been arranged and he meekly canceled the order, with a private smile of amusement. They were all to walk. No one, it seemed, considered it ungenteel to turn up at church with reddened cheeks and noses and snowy boots.

The church, Eleanor found, was filled with familiar faces, to most of which she could even put a name. There were the merchants and wealthier tenants whom she had met in the assembly rooms the day of her arrival at Grenfell, the poorer tenants and cottagers whom she had visited either by invitation or as the bearer of baskets of food and medicine, the poorer people of the village and countryside who had been at the concert and party that afternoon, and the carolers.

She smiled about her as she walked down the aisle with her husband to their front pew and found that almost everyone was smiling back. Perhaps, she thought, oh, just perhaps, it was not so bad after all being a countess. She gave a specially bright smile to elderly Mrs. Richards, who had been almost too ill to sit up during her visit the week before.

A Nativity scene had been set up at the front of the

church. The organ was playing and the church bells
were ringing. Eleanor seated herself and breathed in
the atmosphere of Christmas. It was the most wonderful Christmas she could remember, she thought,
though she had always loved the season as the very
best time of the year.

If only . . . She watched her husband's hand as it
reached for a prayer book. But she must not try reaching for the Bethlehem star. She must be content with
what she had. And what she had was very good if she
considered the very inauspicious beginning her marriage had had less than two months before. If only this
amity—this warmth—could continue when Christmas
was over and their guests had returned home, she
would be very content indeed.

Well, almost, anyway.

And yet she felt guilty suddenly. She had just
thought that this was the best Christmas ever, and yet
Papa was not there. He was dead. Gone forever. She
remembered his last hours, when he had been seeing
and talking to her mother. He was gone and yet she
was enjoying Christmas less than two months later—
as he had requested.

There was an ache and a tickling in the back of her
throat suddenly and she swallowed against both. The
Reverend Blodell was ready to begin the service.

Many members of the congregation stood outside
the church for well over half an hour after the service
had ended and fifteen minutes after the bells had finished pealing. Everyone, it seemed, had to greet everyone else and shake hands. The earl would not have
been surprised to find that all the inhabitants of the
village and its surrounding farms had been invited back
to Grenfell Park. But it was not so. And finally they
were walking home.

There was a great deal of exuberance of spirits.
Some throwing of snowballs. Susan got herself tossed,
shrieking, into some soft snow beside the driveway by
a gang of cousins and Lord Charles. There were, of

course, the laggards. George and Mabel and perhaps Lord Sotherby and Muriel, who had been walking with them when they left the village. Sir Albert and Rachel.

The earl wished he could lag behind with his wife, but it did not seem quite right to wait until everyone else had walked on out of sight merely so that he could draw her against him to kiss her with all the stars of Christmas overhead. He would have to wait, he decided, until the night. At least he had that advantage over the unmarried couples.

"Did you know that Sir Albert talked privately with me this afternoon?" Eleanor asked him suddenly.

"He asked in my hearing," he said, looking down at her.

"He apologized to me," she said, "for his shabby behavior two years ago."

"Ah, did he?" her husband said. "I am glad. You have not liked him, have you, Eleanor? Will this help?"

"Yes," she said. "I am no longer embarrassed to catch his eye. Why did you hit him?"

"Did he tell you that?" he asked, frowning.

"No," she said. "But people who run into doors do not usually have bruises beneath their jaws. Unless it is a very low door. Why did you do it?"

He shrugged. "I will leave you to make your own interpretation," he said.

"He told me something else," she said. "Something that I think you were trying to tell me last night when I stopped you. They really were not your debts, were they?"

"They were appallingly large," he said, "and some of them to moneylenders before your father bought them all. I had no experience in dealing with debt."

"So," she said quietly, "neither of us had a particularly base reason for marrying the other, did we?"

"Except," he said, "that I suppose it is never right to marry solely for money or solely to please a father."

It was the wrong thing to say. He knew that even as

he was speaking the words. It was a downright foolish thing to say.

"And so," she said, and he could hear the strain in her voice, "all the blame is to be laid at my father's door. He is the one who bought your debts and gave you very little choice of action. And he is the one who persuaded me to follow his wishes. All you and I have been guilty of is weakness of character."

"I suppose so," he said after a pause.

"He is to blame, then," she said. "But we are the ones left alive. There was really no basis for a workable marriage, was there?"

Her voice was bleak. But a little pleading? He was on the point of agreeing with her. Certainly she was right. There had been no good basis. Quite the contrary, in fact. Their marriage should have turned out quite as badly as he had expected from the start. But for all that it was not turning out that way. Somehow, though all the odds had been against them, they were making something workable of their marriage after all. It now seemed to have all the ingredients necessary for contentment and perhaps even happiness.

No, he could not agree with her. But of course, she did not want him to. She had asked the question in the hope that he would contradict her. Yes, she had. He knew her well enough now to recognize that. She wanted a good marriage, just as he did.

"No, there was not," he said, "but . . ."

But Aunt Beryl and Aunt Ruth had slowed their pace and drawn level with them.

"Ruth is a little breathless," Aunt Beryl announced in her usual forthright manner. "You will not mind if she takes your arm, my lord?"

"Of course not." He drew Aunt Ruth's arm through his free one and looked down at her in some concern. "I should have had the sleigh come to pick you up at church."

"Oh, no, no," she said, flustered. "I am quite sure the fresh air is good for me, my lord. And such beautiful weather. And such a wonderful service. Was it not, Ellie?''

"It was," Eleanor agreed. "Very wonderful, Aunt Ruth."

"I was just saying to Beryl," Aunt Ruth went on, "that I wish we could have the Reverend Blodell in our parish. Such an imposing figure of a man."

The earl smiled and took up the conversation. But he was going to have to complete that other conversation before bedtime, he thought. Otherwise he was going to find himself in bed with either a marble statue or a hedgehog. The thought fueled his smile.

"Bristol," Viscount Sotherby said to Muriel, finding himself unexpectedly alone with her after their footsteps had lagged with George's and Mabel's until finally that couple had made it quite clear that they would be very happy to lose themselves among the trees for a few minutes. "It is a place I do not know. Is it attractive?"

"I like it," she said. "We moved there from the country after Papa died."

"Perhaps," he said, "I shall pay it a visit when spring comes. Especially now that I know some people who live there."

"That would be pleasant, my lord," she said.

"Did you know I had been married?" he asked her.

"No." She looked up at him with widened eyes.

"She died," he said. "In childbed a little more than two years ago. I would have had a daughter. I was fond of my wife."

"Oh," she said, "I am so sorry."

He smiled. "Fortunately or unfortunately," he said, "grief fades and life goes on. But I liked being married. I liked the comfort and security of it. The bachelor life does not much suit me, I am afraid. I came here to shoot, expecting a somewhat bleak Christmas. What a treat it has been to be part of a family Christmas after all."

Muriel smiled. "I cannot imagine Christmas without family," she said. "Or life, for that matter."

The driveway was deserted, George and Mabel having disappeared among the elm trees. And no self-respecting male could be expected to be alone with a pretty girl under the stars and not kiss her.

Lord Sotherby kissed Muriel.

"Bristol in March," he said when he raised his head. "Will there be primroses?"

"And daffodils," she said.

A promise that was rewarded with another kiss.

George and Mabel and the viscount and Muriel had perhaps lagged behind most of the family, but not as far behind as Sir Albert Hagley and Rachel.

"The stars," he said, looking up. "They seem so close that one could almost imagine reaching out to pluck one."

"My star is still there tonight," she said, looking up with him. "It is even brighter than it was last night."

"That one?" He pointed to a star close to the moon. "That is not your star. It is ours."

"Oh, is it?" She turned her head to smile at him and he released her arm in order to set his own about her waist and draw her closer to his side.

"You have sometimes avoided me recently," he said.

"Yes," she said. "And you have sometimes avoided me."

"For the same reason?" he asked.

"I think not." She smiled gently. "I was told you were a rake, though I do not believe it is true. But it is Christmas and a wonderful time for flirtation. Except that I do not believe I am much good at flirtation."

"Why not?" he asked.

"I cannot be fond of someone one day and forget about him the next," she said.

They had stopped walking. "Are you fond of me?" he asked.

"That is an unfair question," she said, her gaze dropping to his chin. "I think perhaps we should not be alone."

"Because I might kiss you?" he asked.

"Yes, because of that," she said. "And because I am no good at flirtation."

"I am not sure I am good at anything else," he said. "I have had you off alone one too many times, have I not? And I am about to kiss you one too many times. Too many if I mean only flirtation, that is. I don't believe I would fancy coming to fisticuffs with your father. I value my teeth a little too highly."

She laughed softly.

"And so I have been at war with myself," he said. "Telling myself with my head to keep away from you, urging myself with my heart to find you out and to take you apart and to—what? Kiss you? Romance you? I am not sure. I am unfamiliar with the language of the heart."

She smiled at him a little uncertainly.

"I think I had better ask for a private word with your father when we return to the house," he said. He grinned briefly. "Before he has a chance to ask for a private meeting with me."

"You have not really compromised me," she said, her voice breathless. "And we would not suit."

"Wouldn't we?" He gazed down into her eyes. "Because I am a gentleman and you are not a lady? I would have agreed without hesitation before meeting you and before seeing Randolph's marriage develop into a love match before my very eyes. Now those facts merely seem rather silly. You cannot be summed up with a label. You are Rachel Transome and I have fallen in love with you. Did I actually say those words? They are the most difficult in the English language to say aloud."

"It is a love match, is it not?" she said. "I worried when I first heard of it. I was afraid that Ellie had been blinded by the splendor of marrying an earl. And she is my favorite cousin. But splendor has nothing to do with it. When one loves a man, it does not really matter if he is an earl or a countinghouse clerk.''

"Do you speak from experience?'' he asked.

She nodded. "Or a baronet,'' she added.

"Then I will speak with your papa tonight,'' he said. "May I?''

She nodded again.

There was that deserted driveway again. And those stars again. The interview with Uncle Ben would have to wait for a while until Sir Albert had finished kissing Rachel quite thoroughly. And then they had to smile at each other and tell each other again what they had said quite clearly before.

And then the new declarations had to be sealed with a kiss.

Unknown to anyone except Aunt Catherine, Uncle Harry had brought large amounts of champagne with him to Grenfell Park. He had his valet bring them down to the drawing room when everyone had finally returned to the house. It was after midnight, yet no one seemed inclined to go to bed, except perhaps Tom and Bessie, who explained that their children were likely to be up before the lark in the morning.

"I brought it, you see,'' Uncle Harry explained, "to accompany an announcement that Catherine and I planned to make on Christmas Day jointly with Beryl. No one, of course, will have guessed what the announcement is to be since the two young people concerned have shown no particular preference for each other during the past few days or indeed during the past two years.''

Mabel blushed and George half smiled as everyone laughed.

"It is a betrothal announcement, you see,'' Uncle Harry said, "between our George and Beryl's Mabel. And so our families are to be linked by one more tie, the first having been between Catherine's sister and

Beryl's brother. Ellie's mother and father, may God rest their souls. Before the tears flow and the squeals and hugs begin, then, let the champagne be brought on.''

Tears flowed and the squeals and hugs began and the jokes and the teasing too, so that the newly affianced Mabel was soon blushing rosily and George, grinning sheepishly, came to set an arm about her shoulders.

"The wedding is to be in April on Mabel's nineteenth birthday," he said in answer to a question from Cousin Aubrey. "And I want to say a public thank-you here to Uncle Joe, though he is no longer with us to hear me, for continuing to invite us to family gatherings even after Aunt's passing. For if he had not, Mabel and I might remember each other now only as very small children."

And then the champagne was being passed around and toasts were being made and drunk to the betrothed pair, to their parents, to Christmas, to good fellowship, to whatever anyone could think of that would achieve an enthusiastic burst of consent and a clinking of glasses.

Uncle Sam finally got to his feet and waited until there was silence, not an easy achievement under the circumstances. He was looking large and imposing and unaccustomedly serious.

"One more toast," he said. "Ellie was very emphatic in her letters to all of us, and none of us could doubt, having known Joe, that the instructions came from him and not her. We were to leave off our mourning, she wrote to us, and to come here to enjoy Christmas as we had never enjoyed it before. We have done that." He turned to nod at Eleanor, who was seated on the arm of Aunt Ruth's chair. "Yes, we have done that, lass, thanks to you and thanks to the hospitality of your new husband and thanks to his friends and this house. There has never been such a Christmas as this, and Christmas Day still to come."

There was a murmur of unusually subdued assent from his audience.

"But we have to remember for all that," he said. "We are having this Christmas for Joe, because it was his final wish. Let us remember, then, that it is for him, and that he was the finest brother and uncle and cousin and father in the whole world. And we miss him." He raised his glass. "We miss you, Joe."

Aunt Beryl and Aunt Ruth raised handkerchieves to their eyes. Everyone else raised glasses.

So, the Earl of Falloden thought, if he had been left in any doubt, it was all banished now. The strange absence of mourning clothes, the merrymaking when there should be only sober grief, were all Mr. Joseph Transome's idea. Eleanor and the rest of the family were merely keeping a promise made to a dying and beloved man.

A Christmas promise.

He looked across the room to his wife, who had neither a handkerchief nor a glass in her hands but had them clasped on her lap. Aunt Ruth was patting them with her free hand while the other still dabbed at her eyes.

Eleanor was the marble statue again. Totally without color or expression or motion. Her eyes gazed down at her hands. And he understood finally and in a flash. He understood why she had shown no reaction to the straw outside her father's door and the wrapped knocker the morning after their wedding and why she had not rushed upstairs to her father but had stood warming her hands at the fire even when the doctor had come into the room. He understood why she had shown no emotion at all when announcing to him her father's death. Or the morning after. Or on the day of the funeral.

He understood that her feelings were too deep and too terrifying to be expressed. The marble statue was marble only in a very thin veneer on the outside. Beneath she was all warm, loving woman.

Conversation resumed, subdued at first, and gradually grew in cheerfulness. Tom and Bessie took themselves off to bed. Wilfred flirted with Susan and crossed the room with her to the pianoforte. Several other cousins followed them there. Sir Albert spoke quietly with Uncle Ben and the two of them left the room.

Eleanor too slipped quietly from the room without a word to anyone. Perhaps only her husband saw her go. He waited for a few minutes before going after her.

16

The ache was there again and the heavy depression
and the terrible grief. Terrible because she still could
not cry, though she thought she would and stood still
outside the drawing room, her hands over her face,
waiting for the tears to come. But it was too late. She
had allowed her father to die without grieving properly
for him, and now she could never do so.

The finest father in the whole world, Uncle Sam had
just said. Yes, he had been. For all his busy efforts at
running his business and amassing his fortune, she
had always been at the center of his life. There had
always been time for her. And smiles and hugging
arms and love.

*We miss you, Joe. I miss you, Papa. Oh, how I miss
you. How I miss you.*

But she could not cry. She turned to the staircase
leading up to her room. She did not want to go there.
She went downstairs and paused outside the library,
then went on to the conservatory instead, taking a
branch of candles with her. Perhaps the plants and the
long windows facing out to the stars would soothe her.
Perhaps they would help her to cry.

But the plants looked only gloomy in the frail light
of the candles, and the starry night beyond the windows merely made her feel even more lonely. She felt
alone with the vastness of the universe. She set the
candles down and hugged her arms about herself. It
was chilly in the conservatory.

She wished there were other arms to come around
her. She remembered wishing the same thing the night

her father died. But there were no other arms. Oh, Uncle Sam's or Uncle Ben's, perhaps. Either of them would hold her tight if she gave only the merest hint. But it was other arms she wanted. They would come about her later, no doubt, when she was in bed. And there would be the further comfort of the weight of his body and his penetration of her own. But that was not how she needed him now.

She bitterly regretted the gamble she had taken on the walk home from church—if gamble were the right word. Certainly it had not been a considered one, but one taken on the spur of the moment. At first there had been the relief, even joy, of knowing that neither of them had entered the marriage quite as cynically as both had thought at the start. But then had come the suspicion that he must blame her father, that he must hate him. And then the realization that despite everything it was a marriage that should never have been made.

Except that she had grown very quickly to value her marriage, to realize that it was what she wanted more than anything else in life, That *he* was what she wanted more than anyone. She had fallen in love with him very quickly, considering the hatred she had felt at first. And now he was everything in the world to her. He *was* the world. And Christmas and the Bethlehem star too.

But then had come the gamble. She had voiced her doubts, expecting him to confirm them, willing him to contradict her, to assure her that for him too this marriage was important, necessary even. But he had simply agreed with her. Oh, he had been interrupted by Aunt Beryl and Aunt Ruth, it was true. He had been going to say more. But the few words he had spoken had been enough.

Their marriage to him, then, was still something only to be endured, something to be made the best of. He was good at making the best of it. His inherent courtesy as a gentleman, she supposed, had helped him come to a workable relationship with her. But there was nothing more than that. No real affection. Certainly no love.

She wished she had left well enough alone. She wished she had left her dreams intact. She sat down on a chair and spread her hands on her lap. All was leaden and dead inside her. Christmas was gone.

And then the door opened and closed quietly behind her and he came close enough for her to see him set down another branch of candles and a package, although she did not look up.

The conservatory was a little brighter. And seemed a little warmer.

He had expected to find her in tears, though he was not surprised to find the marble statue instead. She did not look up when he came into the conservatory or show any sign at all that she was aware of his approach. She was sitting and staring at her hands.

He remembered his hesitation the evening her father died and she had come down to the salon to announce the fact to him. He remembered wondering what would happen if he went to her and put his arms about her. But at that time he had been unbelievably foolish and insensitive. He had concluded that she was without feelings, that she would resent being touched. And so he had not touched her.

He knew now that he should have done so, hostile as she was to him at that time. She had needed a human touch. By denying it to her, he had perhaps done her irreparable harm. He had denied her a necessary outlet for her grief. And he knew now that there had been grief. That there *was* grief.

He went to stand in front of her and stooped down on his haunches and took her hands in his. They were like two blocks of ice. He chafed them with his own.

"He was a good father to you, Eleanor?" he asked.

"He loved me," she said, her voice leaden. "It is so easy to take love for granted when one has always had it. I knew he loved me as I loved him, but I did not realize perhaps how much until all love was removed.''

His heart felt like a heavy weight in his chest.

''That was why I wanted a child,'' she said.

Her hands were beginning to warm just a little. ''There will be a child,'' he said. ''Children. There will be love in our home, Eleanor.''

''Yes,'' she said.

''You have been unable to cry?'' he asked her.

For the first time she looked up at him, fleetingly. ''Yes.''

''That is my fault,'' he said. ''If I had held you the night your father died, you would have cried then, would you not, and the healing would have begun.''

''We hated each other,'' she said.

''Perhaps,'' he said, ''if I had held you and you had cried we would have hated each other less. Perhaps we would have come to like each other sooner.''

''Do we like each other?'' she asked.

''Yes,'' he said. ''We do.''

She shrugged her shoulders and looked up at him again very briefly.

''I think your father realized how much you would miss him today and tomorrow,'' he said. ''He arranged consolation for that too. Your father was clever at arranging things, I think.''

She looked up at him and her eyes held on his.

''He left a Christmas gift for you,'' he said, ''and a letter. He asked me to give them to you on Christmas Day. It is Christmas Day now.''

Her lips parted, though she said nothing. Her eyes filled with longing and pain.

''Which first?'' he asked.

She swallowed. ''The letter,'' she said.

He handed it to her and watched her break the seal with hands that trembled. He watched her as she read. She held the letter in her lap for a long while after she had finished and then held it out to him, looking briefly into his face.

''My dearest girl,'' he read, ''perhaps you will hate

me by the time you read this, and so I feel the need to justify myself from beyond the grave. I have not much time, Ellie. I want your happiness more than I want anything before I die. I want you married to the right man as I was married to the right woman. You think Wilfred is that man. He is not. If he were, I would give you to him with my blessing. I thought perhaps my judgment of his character was unjust. I thought perhaps it was just jealousy of a man who was trying to take my daughter away from me. So I played a trick on him, Ellie. Forgive me! I offered to buy him a partnership in his shipping company if he would give you up. If he had refused, he would have had the partnership and you. As it is, he has only the partnership.

"Perhaps I should tell you now while I am still alive. But now you would be blinded by hurt. Perhaps you will be anyway as you read this. I can only hope that by the time you do, a tenderness for your husband will have replaced a puppy love for Wilfred. I chose him with care, Ellie, and am only sorry for the coercion that lack of time has forced me to use on him. He is a man of good character and good intentions. He will look after you, out of conscience and honor if nothing else. But I trust that by the time you read this there will be something else too. I think there will."

The earl looked up at his wife. She was looking down at her hands spread in her lap again.

"Don't grieve too much, Ellie," her father had concluded. "I will not pretend that I have wanted to die. And yet as the time approaches, I find myself more and more eager to rejoin your dear mama. I have missed her. Part of me is missing and I am going to be complete again. Happy Christmas, my darling girl. We will be watching you from somewhere up there among the stars, your mama and papa."

The earl folded the letter carefully and set it back down. *"Are* you badly hurt?" he asked quietly.

"About Wilfred?" she said. "I think I would have been more so if he had not come here. It was in bad taste to invite himself here and to expect me to be with him and to talk with him and to love him as I have always done. I have been disillusioned with him and angry with him.''

''But still in love with him?'' he asked.

There was a short silence. Then she shook her head. ''No,'' she said in a whisper. ''And now I am glad I am not. Papa was right about him. Papa had an annoying habit of always being right.''

''Always?'' he said, but he would not allow the hope to show too clearly in his voice. This was not a moment for him but for her. He must give her back what he had deprived her of at the time of her father's death. He picked up the package and set it in her hands.

''It is jewelry,'' she said as she unwrapped the package and opened the box inside. ''Gold. A locket and chain.'' She lifted the locket into her hand and pressed the catch on one side of it. And sat looking down at the two miniatures inside.

He ached for her but waited for her to react in some way.

''It is the portrait of Mama that he used to wear about his neck,'' she said. ''I looked for it after his death but could not find it. And a portrait of himself that he must have had painted recently. Though before he grew so thin.''

He smiled at her, though she did not look up.

''Papa,'' she whispered. ''It was so painful to watch him lose all his weight. His eyes became so large.'' She looked up then, her own eyes large and luminous. ''Do you think he is with her? Do you believe in an afterlife?''

''Yes.'' He nodded.

''Papa.'' Her hand trembled as she looked back down at the portraits and closed the locket, holding it in the palm of her hand. Her lips were trembling too, he saw, and her shoulders.

He took her hand in his, opened her fingers gently, and took the locket. He spread the chain and placed it over her head and about her neck. He had not seen the portrait of her mother, but he suspected that Eleanor must look like her. No one else in the Transome family had her dark red hair, though Jane Gullis did. No one else had her green eyes.

He got to his feet, took her by the elbows, and drew her up with him. And into his arms, which he closed firmly and warmly about her. He felt her trembling give way to shaking. And then the tears and the sobs, deep, painful, heart-wrenching sobs. His own eyes stung and his throat ached, but he held onto her, rocking her in his arms, crooning to her, murmuring words that he could never afterward remember. Pouring his love and his strength into her with every ounce of his will.

At first she thought that the pain and the agony would tear her in two. She could not bear to look at that miniature likeness, so accurate in portraying him as he had been before the ravages of his illness had changed him. She could not bear to think that he was gone forever, that she would never see or talk with him again. Never hear his voice again.

But then the pain eased, almost as if it were flowing away with the tears. And there was comfort and warmth. There was something holding her to life, something assuring her that she must let her father go, that there were other people to live for, other people to love. A leftover sob shuddered out of her and she turned her head to rest her cheek against his damp shoulder. She closed her eyes. She felt more at peace than she had felt for a long time.

"This is a fine way to behave on Christmas Day," she said.

"Yes, it is," he said. "Saying good-bye to a father you loved dearly is a good thing to do at Christmas. Better perhaps than in November."

She raised her head, the back of her hand against her nose. "How can you understand and be so kind?" she said. "You have every reason to hate him. I must look a dreadful fright. And my nose is running."

He took a large linen handkerchief from a pocket,

nudged away her hand, which would have taken it, and wiped her eyes and her face gently with it. Then he gave it to her so that she could blow her nose.

"Rather red," he said, his head to one side, regarding her with a smile that suggested nothing but gentle kindness. "But still very beautiful. Do you feel better?"

She nodded. "Yes, I really do." But she felt a little bereft without his arms about her. She looked at him wistfully. "Did you mean it when you said that we liked each other now?"

He smiled and nodded.

"It was dreadful at the start, was it not?" she said.

"For which we must both take the blame," he said. "Apart from the fact that we did not know each other and did not want to marry each other, we also both had preconceived ideas about what the other must be like. As if all aristocrats and all members of the business class must be alike. Peas in a pod. Foolish, weren't we?"

"Yes," she said. She hesitated. "Dorothea Lovestone . . ." she began.

". . . is a sweet and helpless and rather dull young lady," he said. "I no longer even think I love her, Eleanor."

"Oh," she said.

"Someone—doubtless Uncle Sam," he said, "has decreed that absolutely no Christmas gift is to be opened until morning. But I want to give you one now, Eleanor. It is not really a Christmas gift since I bought it for you soon after our marriage—out of a sense of guilt, I suppose—but have found myself unable to give it to you. I am glad now that I did not give it sooner, because it would have meant nothing until now."

He reached into a pocket and drew out a package even smaller than that which had held her locket. And she opened the box containing her diamond ring.

"Just a single diamond set in gold," he said. "I felt it was too fine a gem to be surrounded by others. I did not realize at the time that it was very like my wife in that sense.''

She looked up at him, her eyes filling with tears again. He drew the ring from the box and slid it onto her finger, next to the plain gold band that he had put there—reluctantly onto a reluctant finger—on their wedding day.

''Thank you,'' she whispered to him, though she was not sure whether she thanked him more for the ring or for the words. ''It is beautiful.''

''I told you a little while ago,'' he said, ''that there would be love in our home when a child of ours is born, Eleanor. When children are born. But there is more love than just that. There is love here already. I seem to have fallen in love with a hedgehog. I wanted you to know. But you must not be oppressed with the thought. You like me and I think perhaps you are a little fond of me and you want to have and to love my children. That will be enough for me, Eleanor. I will be content.''

She hardly dared believe the evidence of her own ears or her own eyes as they gazed into his and saw the truth there. ''In what way do you love me?'' she asked.

''Ah,'' he said, ''how does one put a measure on love? How does one explain it in words? How do I love you? With my body. With my heart. With my soul. It sounds foolish, does it not?''

''And you will be content,'' she said, ''with less than that from me?''

He smiled at her and bent to kiss her cheek softly. ''I will be content,'' he said.

''Liar!'' she said. ''I would not be content. I would be the veriest hedgehog for the rest of my life. I would give you no peace. I would quarrel with you every day and every night too for the rest of our lives. If you did not love me as I love you. I like your way of describing it. With my body and my heart and my soul I love you, R— Oh, dear, it is so hard to say when I have not said it in a month and half of marriage. I love you, *Randolph*. There, I have said it. I love you.''

They stood grinning at each other like a pair of fools while she felt laughter bubbling and brimming in her and happiness so intense that she wondered how it could keep from bursting out.

And then it did—and out of him too at the same moment, and he had her off her feet and was twirling her about and about until they were both dizzy, and then he was kissing her deeply and more deeply until they were both dizzier.

He set his forehead to hers when the world somehow came whirling back to its center. ''You see?'' he said. ''Your father was right again. Despicable, was he not?''

''Oh, quite,'' she said. ''But how could he possibly know that we would suit? It was hatred at first sight.''

''I have the strange suspicion,'' he said, ''that for once in his life your father gambled quite recklessly. And won. I have a stranger suspicion that his middle name must have been Midas. He certainly touched gold in our case.''

''Randolph.'' She reached up and ran her fingers lightly through his hair. ''Do you think our star is still overhead tonight? Or is it over the stable?''

They crossed to one of the windows and peered upward at the myriad stars above. They were all equally bright. How could they possibly know which star he had picked out the night before? But he pointed to one not quite overhead.

''There,'' he said. ''No longer above us, you see, Eleanor. But it was last night. It has led us to Bethlehem. How did Uncle Ben put it last night? It has led us to peace and hope. And love.''

''Papa wanted us to have a wonderful Christmas for him,'' she said. ''Do you think he realized how very wonderful it would be?''

''I have no doubt of it,'' he said. ''I wonder what time it is. Half past one? Two? Later? If I assure you that heart and soul are still fully involved, Eleanor, would you care to come to bed so that I can show you that third way I love you?''

"Only if I can show you too," she said. "I will never allow you to make love *to* me, you see, Randolph, but only *with* me."

He chuckled. "Happy Christmas, my love," he said.

"Happy Christmas," she said, "my love." And she smiled back at him and set her hand in his.

"Besides," he said, "we have a Christmas promise to keep and what better way to keep it?" His hand closed warmly about hers.